THE BLOOD BAPTISM DUET

SAINT HARLOWE

Copyright © 2024 by saint harlowe

All rights reserved.

No portion of this book may be reproduced in any form without written permission from the publisher or author, except as permitted by U.S. copyright law.

this is a fast-paced dark taboo romance containing a fictional toxic relationship. the romanticization of said relationship is not a reflection of the author's or consumer's ethical beliefs but is meant to be an engaging literary *fantasy* intended only for adults. language and themes present in this story might be troubling for some. please read with intentionality & care. content includes but it not limited to: cannibalism, dubcon, knife play, blood play, primal play, explicit sex, stockholm syndrome, bdsm, gore, abuse, alcohol use, roleplaying, hunt/chase, religious trauma, breath play, gagging, murder, waterworks, fisting, drowning play, forced drugging, abduction, dismemberment

rapture

I WAS TAKEN ON a Sunday. The Lord's Day.

I thought of scripture as I stared at the backside of a beige door. Gold ribboned the frame, disrupted by a dark blur crossing an unknown threshold—once, twice, a third time—until unfamiliar footsteps halted, allowing light to bend around the splintered wood. *On the seventh day, God rested.* I couldn't shake the thought—God growing tired—as I pressed my spine against a cool wall in an almost empty bedroom somewhere I had never been. A place I would probably never leave.

Sometime ago, during a lesson about drug use and gang violence, a statistic flashed across the cheap projector in my health class: *the first three hours of an abduction are crucial* and *one in six runaways are likely sex trafficked.* Four years ago, I hadn't thought much of it. I'd thought about Prom instead. About kissing and being kissed. I hadn't thought about my bland high school syllabus when I'd been taken, either. Not when I'd fumbled my keys outside a dive bar downtown. Not when a warm, wide hand covered my mouth, and not when my focus had slipped. I'd thought of skating, actually. The moment before you fall. How it sounds—blade against ice—and how it feels—the world slipping out from under you—how you instantly panic, bracing for pain. I'd thought *no* and *fuck* and *stay awake* and *scream, fight, do something, anything*—

But I hadn't.

One moment, I'd gasped, thrashed, whimpered, and the next, I'd found myself in a shadowy room, strewn across a mattress fitted with charcoal sheets, willing the blood in my veins to move faster.

Maybe the first three hours hadn't passed yet. Maybe the person outside that door was wearing a badge, coming to my rescue. Maybe I would wake up in my apartment, still a little drunk and shaking from a nightmare. Or maybe I was going to die.

The thought hadn't left me alone. Gliding across a freshly resurfaced rink. Wobbling. Losing my balance. How I could've been at church, but instead, I'd gone for a drink. Whiskey, neat.

That was the thing, you know. The irony.

Sunday was my easy day. My grocery day, my laundry day, my binge-trashy-television day.

It wasn't the day when anything *happened*.

I picked at the edge of my thumbnail, teasing lifted cuticle.

I'm going to die. Part of me knew it was better that way. I wanted it to be over. *Do it fast*, I thought. *Let it be quick*. But the smaller, stubborn part of me who hadn't lived long enough to make peace with death clutched the idea of escape. Bargaining. Rescue. Things most people in my situation never got.

The door wheezed. The lock jostled.

I held myself like a viper, hands pressed to the carpeted floor, calves flexed for flight. I told myself to shoot toward him. *Be unexpected. Be ruthless.* I told myself to become a bullet. But as the hall light bent around the figure in the doorway, I couldn't move. Couldn't breathe, or blink, or speak. My spirit held fast to my bones and my body refused to budge.

The man had a slim mouth. His features were sharp and tactile, like a switchblade. Long, liquid, broad. Alien, almost. The word I was looking for was *athletic*, but his clothes—dark as night—softened his shoulders, whittled his waist, made him look manicured and expensive. He hardly moved, or maybe his movements were too precise to notice. He studied me. *Looked*. And I did the same. Etched his harsh cheekbones and trendy, cropped hairstyle into my memory. Searched for ink and found a crescent moon tattooed on his middle finger. Silver hoops hugged his lobes like faulty fishhooks. Doe-eyed, fair-skinned, deadly handsome. Someone who could get away with murder. Someone who probably already had.

I snapped my teeth when he stepped forward. I hadn't meant to—hadn't tired—but my body descended into a primordial state, disregarding rationality for instinct. My captor did not flinch. He took another step, placing his socked foot an inch from my bare toes, and knelt before me. He rested his forearms casually atop his knees and tipped his head, settling his gaze on my throat, higher, until he met my eyes.

"Are you going to kill me?" I asked. Because what else mattered, really? What else did I have besides that question?

It was a normal Sunday. I'd had my normal drink. I had nothing *normal* left for him to ruin.

Adrenaline seeped into every corner of my being. It jostled behind my ribcage. Buzzed in my marrow. I told myself to lash out. Dig my thumbs into his eye sockets. Kick him between the legs. Crack his neck with the side of my hand. But I still couldn't move.

I went rigid when he reached for me. Sputtered through an inhale as he grasped my jaw and gripped.

"You're Adrian, right?" he asked.

I expected his voice to be rough, but it was smooth as honey. I tried to yank my face away. He held on. "You stole me. You should know."

"Adrian Price," he said, and it reminded me of someone reading from the Bible, peddling faith to nonbelievers. "I'm Jackson."

"Fuck you," I snapped. It was all the bravery I could muster.

Jackson hardly reacted. His eyebrow twitched, and a smile hinted at his mouth—struck through with a scar—but that was all. He released me gently, curious fingers featherlight on my chin, and stood, walking into the hall.

I watched him leave. I listened for the lock.

But like misplaced grace, the door remained open.

If I ran, would he chase me?

The thought ricocheted.

I didn't know where I was. I didn't know where the hallway went, or where I would go from there. If I could find help. If help was anywhere near enough to find.

The door was still open, though. Open and ignored. Open on purpose. Open like an invitation.

I gave the bedroom another once over, checking for anything I could use as a weapon. Soft sheets. A dove white down comforter. An empty nightstand. Nothing else. My clothes were the same ones I'd worn to the bar. Long-sleeved white shirt—cotton, cheap. High waist corduroy pants I'd thrifted a while ago. Ratty sneakers an old roommate had left behind. Plain underwear from a multi-pack: bikini cut, plucked shyly from the women's section at Target.

How long have I been here?

The thought made me pause.

I couldn't remember. Sometime ago, a lifetime ago, I'd lurched awake, groggy and disoriented from whatever inhalant he'd forced over my nose. It could've been minutes. Days. *The first three hours of an abduction are crucial.* I swallowed bile and adrenaline. There was nowhere else to go, though, was there? Dying or living was a predetermined thing. Either I died or I didn't. Either I lived or I didn't.

Purgatory, a third, sacred choice, formed a city between the four blank walls of that bedroom. I could've stayed. Burned. Been kept.

I pushed to my feet, held upright on unsteady knees, and braced against the wall with my palm. Everything beneath my skin felt weak, like someone had removed my skeleton and reassembled it wrong. I righted myself against unfamiliar dizziness.

The apartment, house, *place* stayed quiet until a faucet sputtered. Water flowed from a sink. I pawed at my eyes and took the first step, then another, until my bare toes met the seam where carpet met faux wood in the hallway. *Die, live, stay.* I didn't have a choice—not a real one. Whatever was going to happen had already been decided. I could rage against it. Challenge it. Or move through it. I didn't pray.

Even if God was listening, he'd made up his mind.

"I have green tea and Earl Grey," Jackson said.

I startled and stepped into the hall. I tried not to panic, but my head was on a swivel. I looked behind me. Another closed door. I looked in front of me. To the left, a shadowy, tidy bathroom, and beyond it, Jackson standing in a sleek kitchen, setting a copper kettle on a lit burner. The cutlery block next to the spice rack on the counter caught my attention.

"Adrian," he said, expectantly. I hated how round and full my name sounded in his mouth. "Green or Grey?"

"Green," I choked out.

For a moment, I didn't know how to walk. My legs stayed rooted in place, trembling. I imagined how I'd fit inside a coffin. Being buried in the woods. Where he planned to put me. What he might do to me.

"What do you want?" I asked. I felt like a fucking child, but every time I imagined saying something else—*where the fuck am I* or *scream, scream, scream*—I couldn't place the syllables where they belonged. I thought *let me go* and said, "I'm no one." Told myself to say *I'll make you regret this* and whispered, "Please."

Jackson looked different bathed in manufactured light. The way he'd walked through the bedroom, as if he'd been poured from a bottle, calloused as he moved casually around in the kitchen. His black turtleneck and tailored pants weren't as ominous as they had been a moment ago, when he'd blended in with the darkness, but still, the light did nothing to soften his sturdy, wolfish features. Like most predators, he couldn't hide what he was from his prey, and I recognized every point on his body that said *run*.

Inquisitive eyes. Brown, like sugar melting in a pan. Long, wicked hands. Bones arranged too neatly, too perfectly.

God made mistakes, but the devil didn't. And Jackson's only flaw was a handsome scar.

"Are you hungry?" Jackson asked. He nudged a chair with his foot, signaling for me to sit.

I swayed on my feet. I wasn't, but I said, "Yes." To placate him, maybe. To earn something, anything. A chance. A way out.

"Good." He nudged the chair again then gestured to it with his open hand. "I'll fix us something."

I entered the kitchen slowly, dragging my feet across the smooth tile. My pulse climbed. Everything beneath my skin felt hot and alive. I imagined a deer with a scope aimed at its chest. Rabbits in a laboratory. Caged things. Hunted things.

The area was tidy. A round Ikea table filled the center of the kitchen. On the other side of the hall, a living room with a leather sofa, dark-leafed philodendrons, and a modest flatscreen led to a tiny balcony.

I crossed my arms the way I used to pre-transition, shielding prying eyes from the place where my waist tapered upward.

Jackson grabbed the kettle and tipped its steaming spout, filling one white mug then another. He flicked his eyes from my ankles to my nose.

"No," he said.

"No?"

"I'm not going to kill you tonight."

Tonight. "What do you—"

"Want? That's a complicated question. What do *you* want, Adrian?"

"To go home," I blurted, impulsively, laughably.

Jackson met my eyes again. It was a long, knowing look. The kind that called for honesty I didn't have the strength or bravery to offer.

"Sit," he said, shifting his attention toward the chair. "Do you have any allergies?"

The question bounced like a stone across ice. I wanted to wake up. *Wake up*.

"No." I sat. Sipped my tea. Gripped the mug hard enough to scorch my palm, to remind myself that *yes, awake, yes, alive*. "Does it matter?"

He nodded. "Answer me."

"Shellfish."

He moved with intention. Every step was placed carefully. While he retrieved ingredients from the fridge, I tried to absorb whatever filled my peripheral. I didn't dare take my eyes off him. Not when he placed a skillet on the stove, not when he unwrapped two pieces of meat, not when he chopped vegetables. Popping oil disrupted the silence and the apartment began to shrink, filled with the aroma of herbs and spices.

Run. But to where? I glanced at the balcony. Jackson lived on the seventh story, at least. Lights from Aurora glinted in the darkness, and I realized *night*.

New night.

Dread dropped into my stomach like an anchor.

"How long have I been here?" I asked, trying my best to keep my voice even.

Jackson licked minced parsley from his pinky. "Seventeen hours."

My throat tightened. I stared at the crisp, green liquid at the bottom of my mug and pushed back against the burn in my eyes. Still, a stray tear dampened my cheek. My nasal cavity stung. Everything felt needle-sharp and at a loss. The bright, visceral hope that rescue might come, or escape might present itself ran through my fingers like sand. I thought of Brie Larson picking up the back of a toilet in the movie *Room*. I glanced at the cutlery block. I remembered *Hostel* and *Saw* and every final girl who'd ever perfected their scream. I thought of the people who disappeared every day, in every city, on every continent and never returned.

Adrian Price, another faggot met his maker, another tranny got what was comin'.

"My friends will look for me," I said. They wouldn't. I'd moved three times in the last two years. What they *would* do is squint at their phone when I didn't update my Instagram. Send '*hey nomad u around?????*' when I didn't answer in the group chat. I swallowed hard. "They've probably called the police."

Jackson plated the food slowly. I watched his back pull tight as he drizzled red sauce and sprinkled cheese. He came around the back of my chair and leaned over me, curling his arm around my shoulder. Heat pressed through the back of my shirt. The fine hair on my nape stood.

"You're an independent contractor doing data analytics for start-up companies," he murmured, and set the plate down. "You work remotely, you don't visit your family, and you go to church once a month." He placed his palms on the table beside my dinner, bracketing my shoulders. I held myself like a clenched fist. His mouth hovered close to my ear. "You go to the movies alone. You go to the grocery store alone. You've slept with the bartender at Corkscrew more than once, and you had an affair with a mediocre professor at the junior college where you briefly taught a coding class. If you had friends who gave a fuck, they would've saved you already."

I felt the dimple in my chin, the one that came before a sob. But I held the noise back and rolled my lips together, blinking through blurriness. I didn't trust my voice not to break, so I stayed silent. I didn't trust my hands not to shake either, so I kept them in my lap. *I've been watched. He's been watching me.* The thought stayed suspended in my mind. I replayed bits and pieces of the last week.

Clipper cut at a cheap salon. Had Jackson walked past the window?

The back of Bradley's car after last-call at Corkscrew. Had he seen us?

Drinking a latte at a pastry café across the street from my apartment. Had he been there, too?

Finishing a spreadsheet at a 24-hour diner. Was Jackson one of the night owls I hadn't paid attention to? Someone blatant and ignorable? Someone who'd appeared in my vicinity, someone who'd been in the backdrop?

I cleared the salty phlegm from my throat. "How long?"

"Have I been watching you?"

"How long have you been *stalking* me?"

Jackson took the seat across from me and straightened his shoulders, appearing much more fearsome the longer I looked at him. "A while," he quipped, and dug his silverware into the charred steak on his plate.

Longing for rescue thinned into a hunger for brutality. If I wanted out, I would have to claw my way through Jackson. If I wanted to live,

I'd likely have to kill him. I pawed at my warm, wet cheeks and sniffled, staring hard at the perfectly assembled food on the dish in front of me.

"What is this?" I poked the steak.

"Medium-rare. On the rarer side, to be honest. Leeks, carrots, asparagus, and that..." He pointed with his fork. "...is a sweet potato. There's a cherry wine reduction, too. Sorry if it's a little sour."

Food meant strength. Strength meant endurance. Endurance meant a chance.

I ate the carrots first. Chewed, swallowed, and forced my roiling stomach to keep itself in check. The steak, slathered in butter and perfectly seared, was sliced easily with a dull knife. It went soft under my teeth, like lamb or veal, and I sucked the juice from it on each bite. Copper snuck through the dark, fruity sauce, coating the roof of my mouth. His eyes stayed on me, darting from my plate to the silverware held between my fingers, from my busy hands to my flushed face, following every movement, every mouthful, until I set my utensils down and met his gaze.

"Why me?" I asked.

Jackson pulled the last piece of steak off his fork, scraping his teeth across the silver prongs, and pushed away from the table, standing abruptly. His chair scraped the floor. I winced, but collected myself, inhaling a quick breath as he took my plate and turned toward the sink.

Now, I thought. *Now, go, do it*—

I didn't think it through. Not really. But I wasn't rational enough to sidestep the adrenaline driving my body up and out of the chair. Wasn't clearheaded enough to criticize the decision before it was already in motion. I lunged clumsily for the cutlery block. My palm skated the handle of a potential weapon—gripped, yanked—but the second I'd loosened the blade, Jackson seized my wrist. I screamed because screaming was all I had left. I yelped and thrashed and whimpered as he flipped me around and slammed my hips hard against the counter.

Jackson captured my pulse in one hand and gripped my throat with the other, angling my face toward him. His mean smile deepened, and a wild, newborn ferocity glinted in his woodsy eyes. *Predator*, my brain fired off. *Hunter, predator, warning, alarm, run, get away, danger, danger, danger*. Despite the white-hot rage running through me, I went limp. The heat of him pressed through my clothes, and I begged God to grant me a little mercy.

"We're more alike than you think," Jackson whispered. His raspy laughter sent a chill down my spine. He licked the scar on his mouth and squeezed my wrist until I dropped the knife. "You told your priest about your little daydreams, didn't you? All that shit about the body and blood? The bitemark you left on the bartender?"

I crumbled. Tears distorted my vision and I snapped like a dog, aiming for his cheek. He tightened his grip and hauled me closer, lifting me high, *higher*, until my toes scraped the tile. *Kill me*, I thought. I wanted to say it —scream it—*kill me, kill me, kill me.* But I couldn't breathe. Couldn't do anything except whine and squirm.

"You don't have any secrets, Adrian. I know who you are," Jackson hissed.

Once he relaxed his hold on me, I sucked in a desperate breath. But the relief didn't last. He pulled me through the kitchen, dodged a manic swipe at his face, and shoved me into the bedroom. I tripped. Crashed to the floor.

There he was again, a silhouette in the doorway haloed by ugly, yellow light.

"Maybe I mistook you for a sign from God, but you remind me of Sodom. Pillars of salt, hedonism, holiness," he sighed and worried his bottom lip with his teeth. "I'm not religious, but I'm pretty sure you're my bad miracle."

Before I could yell, or run, or say anything at all, Jackson shut the door.

This time, the lock fastened with a *click*.

I slept fitfully.

Sirens wailed sometime in the early morning. When I peeled my eyes open, sunlight beamed through slots in the blinds, striping the floor. I wound my hand in the comforter and squeezed. *Real*. I turned over on my back and blinked at the ceiling. *Real*. I inhaled, exhaled. Yeah, I was still there. Still a captive. Still trapped in a stranger's apartment, waiting for him to murder me.

I pushed onto my elbows and froze. The bedroom door Jackson had closed and locked last night was wide open.

I glanced around, searching for a trap. The nightstand remained untouched. I slowed my breathing and crawled forward, sneaking a peek around the doorframe. The hall light was off. The kitchen, dark. I stared at the closed door at the end of the hall and imagined Jackson asleep in his bed. Getting dressed after a shower. Shoving his thumb into someone's eye socket, popping the organ free, rolling it around in his hand. I moved quietly, like a church mouse. Pulled myself forward across the floor and scanned the living room for signs of life. Nothing. Another empty room; another deserted place.

Alone. I swallowed to wet my throat and got to my feet, gripping the back of a kitchen chair to stay steady. There, arranged on the table where we'd dined last night, was a stack of folded clothes, a medicine cup containing three pills, and a handwritten note. I looked over my shoulder at the closed door at the end of the hall then picked up the thick, sallow paper. Jackson had clean, tidy handwriting. Small and straight. Like square castles scrawled across dotted lines.

Good morning, Adrian,

Take your vitamins, please: magnesium for your migraines, a multi-vitamin, and zinc. You're welcome to check the bottles in the cabinet if you're uneasy about their purity. Feel free to any of the food in the fridge, but please don't touch the meat in the freezer. If you'd like to take a bath, salts and bathbombs are underneath the sink in the bathroom.

If you try to leave, I'll know.

Yours, Jackson

I set the note down and looked over the clothes he'd left for me. An off-white cashmere sweater, brown pencil pants, and... I ran my thumb along the cotton thong. Heat scaled my neck and filled my face. Of all the things I'd considered, *that* hadn't been one. Surely Jackson had abducted me for something more sinister than pleasure. But last night... The way he'd trapped me against the counter and wrapped his hand around my throat. There was something intimate about it. Something disgustingly provocative.

I wanted to fill a syringe with bleach and plunge it into my ear. Soak my brain until it stopped being fucking *sick*. I didn't want him. I could never want him. But the idea that *he* wanted *me*—that I was alluring enough to be hunted, followed, memorized—settled in my chest like a hot stone. I thought of drowning. I dug my thumbnail into my palm and rushed toward the front door, scrabbling at the deadbolt. Mania made me into a monster. I twisted the doorknob. Pulled hard on the chain-lock and scratched at the smooth, onyx-colored surface. *Out*, I thought, *let me out, let me out, let me out.* It was no use. The door didn't open. The building remained silent. I smacked my forehead against the door out of frustration.

In small font, two lines below a major headline, the Aurora news might broadcast: *Adrian Price, twenty-two, found dead in an apartment with a black door.*

I squeezed my eyes shut. Centered myself. I could scale the balcony and try to get into a neighboring apartment. But if I fell, I died. I took heavy, fast steps into the kitchen and yanked open drawers, revealing Tupperware, silverware, and clean dishes. Every knife in the cutlery block had been removed. I stopped again. Inhaled until my lungs burned. Exhaled as slow as I could. I strode down the hall and twisted the knob on Jackson's bedroom, surprised to find it unlocked. Adrenaline sent me stumbling into the darkness, greeted by bookshelves, a large bed in a low frame, and the subtle scent of citrus cologne.

I stood in the threshold between hallway and bedroom for a long, long time. Everything looked normal. His bed was tidied and topped with a forest-green comforter. Paperbacks and hardcovers filled the shelves alongside candles shaped like Greek statues and various animal skulls. The lamp on his nightstand had a beige canvas shade, looming over a nondescript book and a glass half-filled with water. I imagined him occupying the space. Lending comfortable touches to items and trinkets. Flipping through twice-read pages. Fluffing his pillows.

At what point had he decided I would be taken? Had he been lying in that bed, mulling over his options? Pacing in front of the window, recalling my route home?

My transparent reflection on the window across the room was distorted and strange. I hugged myself, holding onto my elbows, shoulders rounded toward my ears, I looked bony and undone, like a feral cat unused to being housed. I felt like one, too. Jittery and strange. Unable to shake my anxiety or parse my stampeding thoughts.

I walked backward, taking slow, soft steps until my shoulder was parallel with the bathroom.

I deserved to be clean. I deserved to feel some semblance of normalcy.

I grabbed the clothes off the table and walked into the bathroom, clutching the outfit to my chest as I peeked into the glass-walled shower, looked over the edge of the rectangular bathtub, and scanned the vanity. I opened the medicine cabinet and found a toothbrush, still wrapped in new packaging, and a fresh tube of toothpaste. Underneath the sink, a few individual bathbombs filled a wooden tray next to a bag of maple-scented Epsom salt. I set the clothes on the vanity and closed the door. The button-lock refused to stay in place. It made an empty, windy noise, popping open whenever I pressed on it. My throat itched.

The shower ran hot, spewing from a large panel. They were called rainforest showers or some shit like that. Ridiculous, rich people playthings I'd never had the pleasure of experiencing. Fancy shampoo and conditioner in sleek, spaceship-shaped bottles stood inches apart in the inlaid shelves. Primrose soap left my skin buttery and sweet. I used the razor, shearing stubble from my legs and between my thighs. Wrapped in steam, alone and surrounded by neutral sound—water pelting tile, pipes humming—I found a sliver of peace. I became myself again for the smallest, fragmented moment, but once I turned the water off and stepped out of the shower, I was trapped again.

I swiped my hand across the steamy mirror. I had never been muscular, but the impossibility of my own feebleness stared back at me like a nightmare. Birdish and lithe were kind words. Pink scars curved beneath my pectorals, and I had a long, lean torso, leftover from the womanhood I'd forcibly outgrown. The heat reddened my cheeks. *Like apples,* Bradley had said once. We'd fucked in his car on his lunch break. Smoked cigarettes and kissed lazily. *You have a face like one of those painted angels.* He'd meant cherubs, but I'd nodded anyway, cupping my hand between my legs to catch what he'd left inside me.

I raked my fingers through my hair. Wheatish. Plain. I'd never had the courage to dye it chestnut or auburn or any of the colors I loved on other people. I replayed that memory. Riding Bradley in the backseat of his beat to shit car. Drunk, post-confession, still scented like church and whiskey. I'd imagined mastication. My teeth in his stomach, around his ribs, sinking deep into his core. Chewing on his insides, absorbing what he had that I didn't. Freedom, nonchalance, humor, an Adam's apple. I put two fingers to the dent where my clavicles bent, creating space for my sternum.

Blue-eyed, like my mother. Full-lipped, like my father. They'd raised me Catholic, like their parents had raised them.

But I'd extracted myself like a splinter from their lives, and now I wondered what my obituary might say if anyone took the time to write one.

Ma'am, your son is dead, the police would say.

Confused, bewildered, standing on the porch, my mom would flap her lips. *I don't have a son.*

The scene played out, cartoonish and far away. I didn't want to think about her. I didn't have time to hyperfixate on the inevitabilities I wouldn't be around to mitigate.

I took a towel from the shelf above the toilet and dried off. Dressed in the fresh clothes Jackson had chosen for me and watched myself unblur in the mirror as the steam dissipated. My hair fell over my brow. I pushed it out of my face and sighed at myself, swathed in something a cute academic would wear. Pretty, untrained pet. I chewed on the inside of my cheek. Like a fox or a lynx. I brushed my teeth and kicked my dirty clothes into the bedroom where Jackson kept me. I'm not sure why I did it, as if any of *his* space was *my* space, but it felt like the appropriate thing to do.

After that, I walked down the hall and entered his bedroom, ignoring a burst of nausea and the quake in my legs.

The literature on his shelves—high fantasy, dark academia, theology, and biology—were well-loved. I picked up a skull. Rabbit, maybe. Turned it over in my palm and felt across the jagged edges of tiny, preserved bones. Framed butterflies and various taxidermy bats hung on the wall. I dragged my finger along the glass protecting them from the world and paused in front of the open entryway to an attached bathroom. Nice shower, just like the one I'd used, and a couple's vanity. I perused his closet. Gripped the sleeve on a leather jacket. Put my fingerprints on his button-downs and cotton Henley's. Smothered my face against his black denim and licked the collar on his wool coat. He'd taken me, but *someone* would find out. Any cop worth a damn would know.

In the back of the closet, a small, black dresser with glossy drawers hid behind clothes on hangers. I opened the top drawer and my stomach leaped into my throat. Tools. Not tools. Toys. Not toys. Both. Right, yeah, both. Embarrassment flared. I almost slammed the shallow drawer shut. I pulled my hands away instead. Held them against my chest, under my chin, and stared at the glossy, black-handled riding crop. There was a flogger, too. A sleek, silver plug, and a black vibrator, and silk ties.

"Get it together," I said to myself, out loud where I couldn't escape it. "You're a grown fuckin' man."

I'd explored before. Fucked men who liked handcuffs and spanking. Watched porn where people were struck with whips or smacked across the face. But I'd never seen a collection so lovingly kept. I shut that drawer and opened the next. My blush worsened. Another toy—curved silicone with a flared bottom—next to a remote. Neatly bundled crimson rope. I closed the drawer.

Jackson didn't seem like the type of man who had trouble pulling partners. He certainly wasn't ugly. I shifted my jaw back and forth.

What he'd said to me last night stayed branded on my bones. *I'm pretty sure you're my bad miracle.* I stared at the compact dresser and my body went hot, went rigid, did so many things at once I couldn't keep track. My cunt squeezed, my lungs emptied, my head spun.

"No." I spoke aloud again, dislodging the stone from my throat.

Jackson wouldn't abduct someone for sex. He could get that anytime, anywhere.

Whatever he intended to do with me was much, *much* worse.

I left the closet how I found it and stood in front of his bed. Shadows pooled in divots across the rumpled comforter. I thought of him sprawled across it. Reading, sleeping, planning a murder. The mattress dipped under my hands then my knees. I wrapped myself up in the place where he kept warm. Tangled my arms in his comforter, dragged my tongue across his sheets. Reached beneath my waistband and slipped into my underwear, dragging two fingers between slick folds. I wiped myself on his pillow.

Whatever he decided to do, he would find me everywhere after. If he threw my body in the ocean, the police would still find my DNA. If he buried me, an investigator would find flesh, sweat, hair.

I panted against his pillow, scented like aftershave and lemon, and let my limbs turn to jelly. He had a soft bed for a psychopath. High quality linen. I laid there for a while, staring at the book on his nightstand.

I don't know how much time passed, but when a key finally jostled the lock on the front door, I lurched out of Jackson's bed, smoothed the comforter, and darted into the hall. I don't know why. I don't know what I thought I'd accomplish by placing myself outside of his personal space. I heaved in deep breaths and adjusted my stance, posturing confidently.

Jackson locked the door behind him. His dress-shirt and tailored pants hinted at a corporate gig. He wore a black beanie, though, like some kind of skateboarder, and tilted his head, greeting me with an impish smile.

"Look at you, little dove," he cooed, dragging his gaze across me.

"Your neighbor probably called the police. I've been screaming, I—"

"I've been watching," he interjected. He toed off his shiny, pointed shoes and let the messenger bag slung over his shoulder slide to the floor. "Even if you did, no one would hear you. These apartments used to be rent-by-the-hour studios before the new owner bought and refurbished them." He rapped the wall with his knuckles. "Sound-proofing included."

I set my teeth so hard it hurt. "Tell me what I'm doing here."

He jabbed his finger at the table. "Not taking your vitamins, obviously."

My mind misfired. I screwed my lips into a frown. "Why did you take me?" I spoke slowly, annunciating. "What do you want?" But before I could stop myself, I tripped over my own courage. "I—I won't tell anyone. If you let me go, I'll just *go*. I won't say a word, I won't..." I clamped my mouth shut, inhaling shakily through my nose. I wrung my hands, squeezing, rubbing, pulling. "I'm a person," I blurted, shamefully. "You can't keep me. I'm not a kitten you brought in from the rain."

Jackson studied me the same way a zoologist might. His dark eyes flicked here and there, and he lolled his head from side to side. He parted his lips, let out a sight, and gestured to the kitchen table.

"You're not a kitten, no."

"Then let me go."

"No."

"Why?" I laughed, flabbergasted. I'd lost my mind. "You said I'm your *bad miracle*. What the hell does that even mean?"

"Ask me over dinner."

"Answer me."

Jackson leveled me with a stern glare. He opened his messenger bag and retrieved the cutlery, carefully placing each knife back in the block. He moved swiftly, carrying his bag with him through the kitchen, into the hallway, striding straight toward me. I froze. Braced. Made a terrible, pathetic noise and flinched when he brushed past me. He entered his bedroom, dropped his bag, and started to undress. I don't know what I expected. For his knuckles to crack my cheek, for him to throttle me, for him to yell. I gave up on controlling myself and looked over my shoulder. He looked right back at me.

Shirt and beanie, gone. Jeans low on his hips, hugging prominent bone. He wasn't Batman underneath all that black, but he wasn't what I'd expected either. A splatter of charcoal ink decorated his stomach, filling the space beneath his bellybutton. Gothic, sketchy, finely etched, the tattoo resembled bramble or tendrils. I'd seen similar designs on album covers. Horns curved upward from a subtle face, like the skull of an elk. He was lean, toned, fair. Nice arms. Good shoulders. He cracked his slender neck and cleared his throat.

He lifted an eyebrow. "Did you find what you were looking for?"

I held onto what he'd said. *I've been watching*. It collided with *little dove*. I forced my expression to stay neutral. "No," I said. Better to be truthful.

Jackson laughed in his throat. "That's a shame."

He disappeared into the closet and returned wearing a slouchy grey long sleeve and straight-legged jeans. His dark hair, colored like resin, was slicked back, exposing the close shave around his ears. People paid good money for style like that. Apartments like his. The shower, the décor, the clothes… Everything pointed to *rich*. Well-off, at least.

I didn't know what to do with myself. Yesterday I'd been a crying mess, but I couldn't manage to tap into that same panic. My tank was empty. My head hurt; my eyes ached. Jackson walked past me again, crossing the hall into the kitchen. He pushed his cuffs to his elbows. Grabbed a few things out of the fridge and placed a skillet on the stove.

Why bother? I consciously relaxed and followed him. Crossed my arms but left them loose. Stood fully on my feet and leaned my hip against the counter next to the sink.

If he could watch me, I could watch him.

"What do you do for a living?" I asked.

The tendon in his arm flexed. He chopped meat into cubes. "I'm a paralegal."

"How old are you?"

"Twenty-nine."

I narrowed my eyes. "Hobbies?"

He snorted and glanced over his shoulder, furrowing his brow.

"It's a fair question," I said.

"I like to cook."

"And?"

"Test the limits of resilience."

"Resilience?" I hadn't listened closely enough. I should've.

Jackson turned. He rinsed the knife and lifted it, pressing the very tip beneath my chin. The panic I thought had abandoned me resurfaced in an instant. My breath caught. I lifted my face. He drove the knife closer. The point met my skin. Pushed. Gently, like a first kiss. I kept still and stared at his expanding pupils.

"Yes," he said, soft as a bird, "resilience."

I could barely breathe. That knife, close to puncturing. His eyes, ripping me open. "Have you killed people?"

"Yes."

"How many?"

"Does it matter?" He angled the knife higher, scraping the tip up my throat to my chin.

The blade snagged. I winced, hissing between my teeth. Jackson lowered the knife and brought his thumb to the insignificant wound, pressing his digit there. *Don't touch me.* I willed the words to come, but they wouldn't. I stopped breathing, stopped thinking. My entire life narrowed to the place where his skin touched mine. I hated it—that injustice. How he could flay me open without even trying. I didn't know him. I needed to fear him, hate him, *escape* him.

"What's your name? Your full name?" I mumbled.

Jackson brought his thumb, darkened with a red bead, to his mouth. "Jackson Monroe."

"Are you going to kill me, Jackson Monroe?"

His eyebrows twitched together. Surprise looked strange on him. "Not tonight."

I let time expand after that.

Jackson went back to cooking and I touched my chin, applying pressure to the tiny cut. It hardly bled. I created an archive in my mind for everything Jackson Monroe. The freckles on his nape. How veins arced against his fair forearms. His manicured fingernails, tapered eyebrows, and tattoos.

"How'd you get that scar?" I asked.

"Which one?"

"On your mouth."

He plated our food and set the dishes on the table. Spinach fettuccini with cream sauce and burnt ends topped with diced tomatoes. He pulled out my chair then took the seat across from me, knuckling a miniature bowl filled with grated parmesan toward me.

"This." He reached into his back pocket and flicked open a slender knife. The tool was gunmetal. Sleek, clean, pretty.

"You did it yourself?"

"No," he said, like someone would say *obviously*, and twirled his fork in the pasta.

I ate politely, same as him. When he asked if I wanted a glass of wine, I nodded, and when he offered me a choice between two different bottles, I pointed to the cabernet. The food melted in my mouth. Balanced, clean, smoky. The meat, like last night, strung apart beneath my teeth. I hardly chewed.

"Lamb?" I asked.

"Good guess," he said.

"What *is* a bad miracle?"

Jackson paused mid-bite. His lips ticked upward, and he sat straighter, staring at me down his strong, sloped nose. The table was claustrophobically small.

"In Genesis, God placed a pomegranate tree in the center of Eden and called it forbidden. When Eve ate the fruit, freewill was unleashed, right?" He waited for me to nod before he sipped his wine and continued. "And an angel stopped Abraham from sacrificing his son while the child was bound to an altar?" Again, I nodded. "The blind gained their sight, the hungry were fed, Moses split the sea." He waved his hand in a circle. "Miracles were interventions from God. Typically, a show of power from the mighty to the needy."

"Miracles are unexpected answers to unfulfilled prayers," I said, matter-of-factly. Theology wasn't an appropriate arena for an argument—I knew that as well as any other misguided Catholic queer—but Jackson spoke with authority I'd only ever heard at church. It was infuriating. Offensive, even. I don't know why I expected anything else, or anything more.

Jackson took another bite. "Genesis is the story of a bad miracle. Pandora's Box offered on a silver platter."

"And?" I set my utensils down and picked up the wine glass, resting it against my mouth.

"You're the point of contention. Who I am and who I will be are entirely dependent on you," he said, so seriously my muscles locked.

I kept hold of the glass. Cabernet soaked my bottom lip. I met his eyes and waited. My blood thrummed. I had to fight to hear him over the sound of my heartbeat, drumming fast, faster—

Jackson's smile gentled. "You're my Genesis, Adrian. I didn't bring you here to kill you."

"Then why *am* I here?" I lowered the glass. Licked the chalky wetness from my lip.

"To be a merciful consequence or an opportunistic judgement." He shrugged, picked up his silverware, and went back to eating.

"Speak plainly, asshole." I snapped.

One cheek stuffed full, he smiled and gave a close-lipped laugh.

I should've raged. Should've panicked, screamed, and flipped the table. But Jackson simply finished chewing, swallowed, and blotted his lips with a cloth napkin, and I simply sat there, holding my fancy crystalware, trying to parse his biblical riddle.

"Cheers. Are those your only questions?" He reached across the table and clinked our glasses together.

I shifted my jaw back and forth. Annoyance brewed in me, but curiosity churned hotter. "How did you know what I told my priest?"

"I bugged the confessional," he said, nonchalantly.

I gaped. "You bugged the confessional," I repeated, stupidly. "You bugged a church? *My church?*"

He nodded and said, "Uh huh," as he ate, frowning when his noodles slipped off his fork. "Father Hudson didn't seem shocked to hear about your affinity for sleeping with men, or your transition—"

"It's a progressive church."

"Sure, whatever. He didn't give a shit about it," he said, lashes flicking with a stony glance. "I'm surprised he didn't report you after the—" He snapped his teeth, chomping at the air. "—biting incident with Bradley, though."

My cheeks flared hot. It hadn't been an *incident*. I'd... *It hadn't*. Bradley and I had been sleeping together for a while, and I just... I bit him. It wasn't deep. He'd bled a little, but... I averted my eyes to the table and tried to tame my blush. I remembered the tendon in Bradley's neck going taut. How I'd placed my teeth there and let my jaw go heavy, sinking bone into flesh. I'd gone slow. Savored the stretch, pop, break of his skin, and drifted from ecstasy into horror when I'd pulled back to see outright fear in his eyes.

"You told Father Hudson you enjoyed it," Jackson tested. He poured himself another glass then filled my glass, too. "Said it tasted like divinity."

"Blood is holy," I said, and washed the lie down with a sip of fresh wine.

"And your fantasies about consuming Christ? That was a testament to your faith, I'm guessing?"

"It's communion. Stale bread and grape juice."

"Not for you," he said. The words ghosted out, spoken like a secret.

"What? Is it weird to bite in bed now? Did some weeaboo on the internet say it's problematic? Jesus." I gulped the rest of my wine in two mouthfuls. "Why does it even matter?"

Jackson cocked his head, considering. "Because you liked the taste of him."

"*And?*" I gestured around the apartment, swinging my arm dramatically. "I'm eating dinner with a murderer who drugged and kidnapped me. I don't think there's such a thing as *normal* anymore, all right? People like what they like. What else did you do, huh? How else did you *watch* me?"

"I learned your route home from the junior college. Followed you. Studied how you moved, where you went, what you did. When you stopped teaching, I started ordering takeout from the café where you did your contract work." He paused and met my eyes. "You leave your blinds open. You're easy to spot from the fire escape next door to your building. I watched you cook for yourself, water your plants, binge Netflix, get drunk, masturbate on the couch." His thin mouth twitched. "Anyone could've seen you, by the way. Someone else probably did."

I wanted to slap myself. To scrub the bewilderment from my face. But all I could do was stare, slack-jawed and wide-eyed, and endure a headrush from the influx of heat blooming in my skull.

"You're blushing," he rasped.

Embarrassment seemed like such an immature reaction. Jackson Monroe had stolen me. Slapped a rag over my mouth and abducted me. And I was ashamed he'd seen me *masturbate?* Violating, yeah. But unimportant. I steeled my expression and shrugged. Grabbed the cabernet and tipped the bottle upright, pouring what was left into my empty glass.

"Consequence or judgement. Which one do you think I am?" I asked.

Jackson's lips curved. "Judgement."

"Why?"

"Because you're inquisitive." He paused, sliding his gaze to my throat, my chest, then to my hand. I held the glass delicately and told myself not to quiver. The alcohol made it easier to relax, at least. His slow assessment clipped my shoulder, then moved back to my face. "Curious," he said. The word stretched like taffy. "But you might surprise me."

"Consequences are different depending on who you ask. What does it mean for you?" I finished my dinner and wiped my mouth with the back of my hand.

Jackson made a show of looking at my unused napkin before looking at me. "Death," he said, nodding slowly. "Karmic justice."

"And judgement?"

"A decent into unknown territory. Newness. Change."

"So, you brought me here to kill you or, what, *change* you?" The wine made my head cloudy. I was warm, fluid, and brave. "Give me the chance and I'll be your consequence."

"Promise?" Jackson teased, winking slyly.

I hadn't smiled since I'd been abducted. The shock of it—my lips curving—felt alien. I didn't answer him. Instead, I pushed away from the table and turned my back to him, walking briskly down the hall and into the bedroom he'd locked me in last night. The room wasn't mine, but it was all I had. The only place where I could close something behind me and be alone. I put my back to the door and took a deep, grounding breath.

All the questions I'd wanted to ask him rushed at me. *What made you like this? Are you going to hurt me? Did you like what you saw? Do you really think we're anything alike? Am I going to survive you?*

I took off my clothes and crawled under the comforter. Lights from the city glinted through slots in the blinds. Everything, myself included, felt completely out of reach.

THE DOOR OPENED AT a quarter 'til midnight.

Sleeping in a hostile environment meant I was halfway conscious, teetering on the edge of rest. I jolted awake instantly. For the first time, Jackson moved with inexcusable predatory intention. I saw it in his corded arms, held tightly as he lashed out and snatched my ankle. I knew it in his dark eyes, laser focused as I thrashed and kicked, and I felt it in his grip, insistent and mean. He hauled me forward and seized my wrist, yanking me onto my feet. I made a noise I hadn't thought I was capable of making, like a growl but worse, like a whimper but harsher.

I dug my heels into the floor. Jackson pulled me harder. He manhandled me—fingers on my hips, palms heavy on my waist—until we entered his bedroom. In one, single thrust, he threw me onto the bed.

I landed on my front then scrambled to face him, pulling my knees upright to shield my chest, and tried to make sense of my surroundings. Adrenaline was violent and unforgiving, especially when it was the first thing to course through me after dozing off.

Bedroom. Green comforter. Shadowy, silhouetted bookshelves.

My mouth trembled. I swallowed around a jagged lump and willed myself not to cry. I didn't want to give him the satisfaction. Didn't want him to know he'd scared me, or made me weak, or chipped away at my resolve.

"Get on with it," I bit out. "I didn't take you for a rapist, but if this is what you want, get it over with and let me go back to sleep."

"I'm not," he said, matter-of-factly.

I was hyper aware of my body. How much of it he could see. How the white thong he'd picked for me stretched over my hipbones. "You're not?"

"A rapist," he clarified. Jackson's upper half was unclothed. Grey joggers hung low on his hips, accentuating his fine build and the tattoo darkening his abdomen. Without a lamp, I only had the moon to go by. Silver glowed on his wide shoulders. His gaze wandered, probing me. "You came in here today, didn't you?"

I pressed my lips together, exhaling a frustrated breath through my nose.

"Did you really think I wouldn't have cameras recording every inch of this apartment, Adrian? *Really?*"

I said nothing. My own naivety needled me.

"Look, I'll make you a deal... You saw my..." He paused. Laughter rumbled in his throat. "...belongings," he decided. "I want you to give me something in return."

I wilted. "I have nothing for you."

"Touch yourself," he commanded. Confidence radiated through his roughened voice.

Something foreign and hot pulsed behind my bellybutton. "What?"

"You heard me."

"No."

"You told Father Hudson you thought of Bradley's blood whenever you touched yourself—"

I spoke through gritted teeth. "What I said to my priest in the confidence of a confessional is none of your business."

Jackson hummed. "What do you have to lose? Shame, embarrassment, formality, guilt, *law*—none of it exists here." He listed his head, watching me carefully.

I burned under his gaze. I wanted to launch through the window and plummet toward the asphalt. Go to pieces against the cement. But I wanted to stay, too, somehow. I wanted to keep burning. The knot in my groin tightened, and the buzz behind my ribs worsened. It was like I'd swallowed lightning. Like he'd placed a cinder inside me and coaxed it to ignite.

"Touch yourself," he said again, softer.

"How?" I blurted.

"Lie back," he instructed.

I inhaled shakily and did as he said, resting my head on his pillow.

Jackson didn't move. "How do you like to be touched?"

"I don't know."

"Yes, you do."

"Like I..." My skin tensed around my skeleton. Every bit of me was too hot, too eager. "Like I'm worthy."

"Of what?"

"*Being* touched."

"Show me," he said.

I'd touched myself during sex plenty of times. Gone in for the assist, followed a command, asked for something someone hadn't given and delivered it myself. But I'd never stretched myself before someone, open and on display, and let them watch while I got off. Jackson stood at the foot of the bed, stoic and patient. A part of me wanted to resist, but a hungrier, messier part of me wanted to hold his attention. Bend him toward me like a wishbone.

I dusted my fingertips along my clavicles, then swept my hand downward, over my sternum, pressing into the tender, pillowy texture of my stomach. Bone jutted outward from my supple hips, hugged by white cotton. I dug my free hand into the comforter and closed my eyes. Slid my knees apart and slipped my palm beneath the waistband of my underwear, tracing the cleft of my cunt.

"What does divinity taste like?" Jackson asked. His voice was even and quiet, floating through the room like a prayer.

I framed my cock and pinched. "Pennies and rosewater…" The words escaped on a sigh. I reached lower, spreading wetness. Cold air hit my damp panties and chased a shiver down my spine. Like this, strewn before a killer, whispering about blood and ritual, I hardly held back the whine budding in my throat. I swallowed it down. Stayed quiet and massaged myself, slicking my cock with slow, circular strokes.

"Tell me what you think about when you're alone."

No matter how hard I tried to focus on myself, I couldn't ignore him. Heat unspooled in my gut, urging my body to relax, my limbs to go heavy, my lashes to flutter. "What life could be like if we were different."

"Different?"

"If we were all like you. If everyone was like me. If people were gentler or…" I lost myself for a breathless moment. The bed dipped. I teased at my hole, sinking a finger deep, and pressed the heel of my palm against my cock, suspended in pleasure. "…or more brutal. If we were honest."

"Look at me." Jackson was so much closer. He held himself above me, hands bracketing my shoulders, knees on either side of my hips. When I opened my eyes, the scar on his mouth seemed deeper. His face, composed with a serene attentiveness I hadn't expected, loomed above my own. "What would you be if you were honest?"

My back arched away from the bed. I fingered myself slowly, squeezing around my knuckles. My cock throbbed. Everything ached. "More," I breathed out. I wanted him to hold me down. I wanted him to chew through my throat, or crush my ribs, or lock his teeth around my clavicle. I wanted him to kiss me. I parted my lips for another windy, weak sigh. "Worse."

A pocket-knife flicked open.

I furrowed my brow and went completely still, waiting for the inevitable. *This is where I die. In a murderer's bed. Wet and wound tight, like a common fucking whore.* But Jackson took my free hand, placed the knife in my palm, and guided the blade to his throat.

"Go on," he murmured, lovingly, lustfully.

I couldn't move at first. Couldn't think. Couldn't breathe. He pressed on the back of my hand, sliding the knife along the dent at the base of his neck. The soft, vulnerable place between bone and windpipe.

I could've thrust the knife under his chin. I could've cut his throat. I could've jammed the blade into his ear, or skewered his eye, or aimed for his pulse.

"What's it like to be holy?" he asked, and set his hand on the bed again, leaving me to clutch the weapon on my own.

My hips jumped. I withdrew, left myself empty and wanting, and pulled at my cock, chasing the promise of release. I wanted to be filled. I wanted the weight of him inside me, taking up space, stretching me wide. I wanted in an animal way. Jackson was right, the shame was gone, the embarrassment vanished, and all I could think about was being taken, and used, and *coming*.

"I wouldn't know," I said, panting.

I set the blade against his fair flesh and pushed. Jackson's skin split. Blood seeped over the knife's edge and his breath quaked. He exhaled, shaky and undone, and warmth splattered my chin, dripped onto my chest, turned my pale skin red, red, *red*. My panties were soaked. I hated the power of it. How my orgasm was fast and unrelenting. How I bent away from the bed and gasped. How I plunged my fingers inside myself again and whined, jaw slackened, eyes set on Jackson. How my cunt clenched, and my heart raced, and my head spun. I dropped the knife. Jackson shifted forward, placing the shallow cut above my face.

Blood splattered my mouth and pelted my tongue.

I should've killed him.

Why didn't I kill him?

I met his eyes and swallowed. He looked at me thoughtfully, like I was an artifact.

Jackson pushed away from the bed, putting space between us. I caught my breath. Endured the aftershocks and pleasant sleepiness. He stared at me, inquisitive, studious. One corner of his mouth lifted.

"You're special, little dove," he said, speaking certainty into the second word.

"I'm not," I choked out. The shame returned. Again, I considered leaping through the window. My bones would break. I would die relishing the taste of him.

My captor crawled away and walked into the attached bathroom. The shower started.

When he didn't return, I did the unthinkable. Brought my hand to the blood puddled on my chest. Spread it across my skin, coated my hand, and reached into my underwear again, painting my cunt red.

I prayed, too. Asked God to turn away from me. *Don't look, Holy Father. Don't look.*

I HADN'T SLEPT IN Jackson's bed.

Last night, I'd left his room while he showered and cleaned myself up in the guest bathroom. I'd avoided my reflection. Stole sleep in fits and starts. The next day, when I'd finally rallied the courage to leave the guestroom, the apartment was empty, same as it had been yesterday. I found another note on the table, another stack of fresh clothes, and another cup of vitamins.

> *Good morning, Adrian,*
> *Take your vitamins, please. We have reservations tonight.*
> *If you try to leave, I'll know. Be good, little dove.*
> *Yours, Jackson*

The clock on the microwave said 1:03 p.m. I chewed on the inside of my cheek and checked the front door. Locked, of course. I explored the living room, dusting my hand along the couch, touching the wall, the bottom of the television, and the black handle on the sliding glass door. Spring dampened the air, but it was chilly outside. Wind shot upward along the high-rise, and my knuckles whitened around the thick banister separating myself from freedom.

I imagined myself falling. Would my body twirl? Would I scream? I inhaled the clean, mountainous air, and looked out over Aurora, a city pressed against the Rocky Mountains. I willed myself to leap over the edge. *Do it*, I chanted, *do it, do it, do it.* But I didn't—couldn't. I thought of last night... My hand smeared red. Jackson's faint smile and white teeth. My heart, shattered, alive, invigorated.

I heard myself say it—*I wouldn't know*—and left the balcony, locking the slider behind me.

I took the vitamins. Ate two pieces of wheat bread. Scrubbed my teeth in a scalding shower, soaped my body, and lathered my hair. I brushed my teeth again. Three times. The taste of Jackson Monroe still coated my mouth.

For a moment, mania drove me to the brink. I lost a piece of myself, I think. I paced in the hallway, nude except for the knee-high socks he'd left with my outfit. I nibbled my nails. Opened all the blinds, then cinched them shut. Took a drinking glass out of the cabinet and smashed it on the kitchen floor, then panicked and searched for a dustpan, collecting the broken pieces with a broom. I wanted to cry, but I couldn't muster any tears. I wanted to be brave enough to die by my own hand, but I wasn't. I wanted to hate myself for what I'd done last night, but I didn't.

I didn't get dressed. Instead, I walked into Jackson's bedroom, like I belonged there, like it was mine, and snatched the leatherbound journal off the nightstand. I expected blank lines, or scribbles, or notes about his victims. Instead, I found his neat, blocky handwriting spanning page after page. Dates and times. Songs and scripture. I stood for a while, flipping through his thoughts, running my finger along the dents where he'd pressed too hard, but I eventually found myself in his bed again, propped against the headboard, reading.

Was I looking for signs of life? Searching for empathy? Picking through his mind, hunting for an access point to who he'd been, who he was, who he would be?

I turned a page and focused.

> *I am alone in the way most people are alone. How does one move through the world on the cusp of greatness, choosing terror rather than companionship? What does someone become when they routinely slip into a primitive version of who they'd intended to be? I am not lost; I am on a path. I am not wandering; I move with intention.*
>
> *But what is a lion to a wolf? A bear to an elk? A lamb to a coyote? Society was not designed to tolerate me, but I am alive despite it. How is it possible to live, consume, and materialize in a world positioned against me?*
>
> *The universe doesn't half-ass a damn thing, does it? I was created. I am supposed to be here.*
>
> *For some reason, I still believe there's another part of me, walking on two feet, waiting to be found. They will become me, won't they? Eradicate me. Alleviate me. Something has to give. Another person like me will be my own undoing.*
>
> *I am alone in the way most people are alone. Alone and searching. Alone and unwilling to give up. Maybe I will remove my own rib. Maybe I will become God. Maybe I will make my own Eden.*
>
> *Loneliness is a pathetic thing. I'm supposed to be separate from the feeling, right? Outside it.*
>
> *What went wrong? I was made to be immune to it, wasn't I?*

"A lonely psychopath," I mumbled, narrowing my eyes at the page. "How convenient."

I kept reading, though. Digested every egotistical paragraph, scanned every strangely poetic line, and silently cursed Jackson Monroe for being human. For making me see him as a person, as a man with desires, and ambition, and violent habits.

> *She opened easily. I sliced her from navel to nose and removed the juiciest, heaviest organs. I served her heart rare, charred with bok choy, garlic, and chives. I didn't know what to do with her liver, so I put it through a processor with mushrooms and onion. I made lightly breaded meatballs and extracted the marrow from her ribcage for a soup base.*
>
> *Do you think God intended this? Or am I a son of Lucifer? Did another deity will me into being and toss me into the world, hoping I'd entertain the desires of my truest self.*
>
> *I ate her lung raw. It made me sick. I'll be sure to cook it through next time.*
>
> *I stirred her blood into a red (2010) from a Cali vineyard. It was thick and separated quickly, but I drank it anyway—*

I dropped the journal.

Not only was he a killer. My captor.

Jackson Monroe, who'd bled in my mouth, and talked me through an orgasm, was a cannibal.

The leatherbound book weighed like an anchor in my lap. I tried to process what I'd read, but a fever spread through my skull. I couldn't blink away the panicky haze, or calm my roiling stomach, or temper the sweat turning my face dewy. I grabbed the journal and opened it. Flipped through more pages, scanning for clues, for my name, for anything.

> *Adrian Price is a beautiful tragedy.*

My chest tightened. I kept going.

> *I've found him, finally.*
> *Mine.*
> *He doesn't know it yet. He hasn't taken the leap.*
> *What a precious thing: dying by his hand. How complete I might feel with him at my side.*
> *Together.*
> *Oh, God would tremble.*
> *I think about dying every day.*

I shut the journal again and clutched the book to my bare chest.

So, that's what he'd seen in me. That's what he'd commiserated with. Some peculiar, untrue hypothesis that we were somehow similar. I swallowed the bile scorching my throat and fumbled with the book, placing it back on the nightstand. I was nothing like him, I decided. I daydreamed, and I fantasized, and I... I behaved like everyone else. I had intrusive thoughts, and weird nightmares, and shameful desires, and I got caught up in things that I shouldn't. But I wasn't him.

Like Jackson had written in his journal, I'd never taken the leap.

No one ever did, right? Not the majority, at least. People had thoughts, same as me. They watched movies, and wondered, and read comics, and tried to imagine what it might be like. How flesh might come away from bone. How consumable a person could be—how consumable *I* might be.

What would it feel like to be eaten? I'd entertained the thought.

And when I'd stood before Father Hudson, open-mouthed for communion, I'd imagined the arc of a fine throat, the dip of a handsome hip, the bend of a petite wrist. I'd told him that, too. In a dimly lit confessional, whispering feverishly, asking for forgiveness.

And Jackson had heard it all.

I went into the attached bathroom and splashed my face with cold water. I ran my index finger along his toothbrush. The bristles scraped my skin. I imagined it jammed in his mouth, catching pink gums. I splashed my face again and dried with a towel hung neatly next to the shower.

Dying was nothing more than an inevitability at this point. I chose to believe that.

Eventually, I would bore him. He would grow tired of me and hunt for a replacement. Someone more suitable. Someone true to his specifications. I would die; he would live.

Right?

I thought of last night, stretched beneath him like Persephone, drinking the blood of a shunned god.

No. I finally looked at my reflection. *I was doing what was expected of me. It was a performance.*

The lie filled my body, slippery and translucent, but I chased it, nonetheless.

I refused to look at the journal as I left his bedroom. I wanted to. Everything inside me said *pick it back up, keep reading*, but I got dressed instead. The outfit Jackson had left for me was much nicer than yesterday. Fitted trousers and a beige high-necked long sleeve. Cashmere, again. He'd left a leather belt, too, fitted with a bronze clasp, and another cotton thong. I'd forgotten about my gold crucifix—such a trivial thing—but he'd left it, as well. I imagined him unclasping the necklace after he'd drugged me. How he could've broken it with brute force. How he could've broken me last night, too.

I fastened the dainty chain and centered the plain cross between my collarbones.

The routine I'd entertained seventy-two hours ago seemed like a past life. I wanted to get back to it. I wanted to mourn it. But I couldn't seem to picture it. I was stuck in a loop—escaping him, understanding him, killing him—and I couldn't recall the details of how I'd lived before survival became the center of my universe.

I wasn't sure if I could kill him. I didn't think I would ever escape him. I would never understand him.

I met my own eyes in the mirror and thought it all again.

I couldn't kill him. I wouldn't escape him. I'd never understand him.

Children lied to soothe themselves. My old therapist told me that a long time ago.

I unscrewed the lid on vanilla-scented texturizer and raked it through my hair. Took a moment to learn this odd, birdish version of myself—a person I'd never had to know.

Captive, unmoored, floating through purgatory. I hadn't given it much attention: the life I'd been stolen from.

I hadn't considered how little I had until I was standing in that bathroom, lying to my finely dressed reflection. Friends who checked in on Discord. Vacations I never took. Men who kept me a secret. Jobs that bored me. Recipes I never got right, sermons I couldn't relate to, people who weren't looking for me.

Another hard, rigid rock filled my throat. I forced it down and dabbed my lashes with a bent knuckle, catching any tears before they fell.

The front door unlocked, opened, closed.

I straightened my shoulders and chewed my bottom lip, shifting my attention to the corner of the mirror where I saw the hallway and entryway reflected. Jackson set his messenger bag down, glanced into the living room, then removed his shoes and walked into the hall. He didn't startle, but he slowed at the sight of me.

"You're dressed," he said, surprised.

"You said we have reservations."

He gave me a quick once over and arched a brow. "We do."

"You're taking me outside?"

"I am."

"Aren't you afraid I'll run? Scream for help? That someone will recognize me?" I mirrored his action, dragging my gaze from his feet to his face.

His tongue darted out, striking his lip. "No, Adrian, I'm not afraid," he said, and leaned forward, pressing his mouth to my own.

I closed my eyes. I hadn't expected to be kissed so easily. I hadn't expected to kiss him back, either. But he was velvet against me, tender and chaste, and I couldn't help the part of my lips, how I eased under the weight of his breath. When he pulled away, I shivered at the sound of his mouth breaking free from mine and watched him stride into his bedroom.

As if it'd been nothing at all. As if he'd kissed me a thousand times before and would kiss me a thousand times again.

I swayed on my feet. I hadn't flinched. I hadn't recoiled, or smacked him, or barked. I'd allowed it, like I'd allowed him to crawl over me last night. I swallowed.

Who the hell am I turning into?

"Have you heard of Chef Lucas Soto? He's hosting a dining experience tonight. Invitation only..." Jackson paused, retrieving a garment bag from his closet. He dressed in front of me again, peeling away his day clothes and tugging black pants into place, followed by a crisp button-down. The wound I'd left at the base of his neck was red and angry. "Grazing menu, small batch ingredients, homemade mead."

I blinked, taken aback. "We're going to dinner?"

"A fancy fuckin' dinner, yeah," he purred, laughing through it.

I didn't want to smile. I tried not to. "A fancy fucking dinner," I repeated under my breath, keeping my eyes on him while he moved about the bedroom, spritzing cologne, adjusting his belt, pulling on socks. "How many people have you abducted?"

"One."

"How many people have you eaten?" I wanted to pluck the question from the air and chew it up. I imagined myself sprinting toward the window. Falling, splitting at the seams, staining the sidewalk.

Jackson leveled me with an amused stare. "Six. Do you always read people's diaries?"

"Only people who kidnap me."

"Fair. I bought you a coat, but I'm not sure if it'll fit. C'mere."

I lurched forward at first but planted my feet at the last second. I wouldn't do what he said on a whim. "I'm not a dog, Jackson."

He rolled his eyes. "Adrian, sweetheart, will you please try this coat on?" He reached into the closet and flipped a long, wool, butterscotch coat around, holding the hanger with two bent fingers. Sarcasm soaked his voice. "I'd hate for you to catch a cold."

Will you please. I blushed furiously. *Sweetheart*. Those words, how fondly they fell from him, snared me like a foolish rabbit. "I'll go to dinner with you on one condition," I tested, waiting for his bemused smile to come and go. "I need my hormones. I'm on topical and injectable, and you've been watching me for long enough to know I shouldn't skip a dose."

Jackson's smile faltered. At first, I thought he might've been angry, but he gave a curt nod and cleared his throat. "Sure, fine."

"Okay."

"Good." He took the coat off the hanger and held it up.

I took slow steps forward and slid my arms into each sleeve. The coat fit perfectly. The collar stood high and sturdy, framing my neck. I'd never worn anything *chic* before. Not really. Not like that.

Jackson smoothed his wide hands along my shoulders. Gripped. Released. "Do you like it?"

"Is it a gift or a requirement?" I asked.

A soft hum, akin to a growl, rumbled out of him. "You decide."

I shot him a cold glance. "You're keeping me captive in your apartment, Jackson."

He tucked his mouth against my ear. "I haven't eaten you yet," he teased, inhaling against my temple. "Do you think there were people like us living in Sodom and Gomorrah when it burned? Do you think the angel would've blinded us?"

"You, maybe," I said. The lie tasted like sulfur.

"Me, definitely, little dove." He brushed past me, snatched his keys, and opened the front door. "C'mon, if we're late, we'll lose our table."

I followed him out of the apartment. Before I could run, or scream, or call for help, he took my hand.

Our knuckles buckled together. The heat of his palm melted into me. He held on, not too tightly, but firm enough to make me blush.

Oh, no, I thought, miserably, delightedly. *My heart is a traitor.*

Chef Lucas Soto rented an old logging factory for the exclusive dining engagement. Palm-sized sportscars and electric vehicles lined the gravel parking lot, blotting the cool landscape neon orange, candy-apple red, lovebird green. Cabins stood on stilts behind the treeline, yellow windows staring outward like eyes, unblinking and attentive, watching high class diners entertain themselves over a ridiculous meal.

I'd started taking mental notes the moment we'd left Jackson's apartment. Eighth floor. Elevator at the end of the hall, no key-code needed. No doorman in the lobby. The parking structure, attached to the left of the building, was half-empty and ominous. Jackson had unlocked a sleek, pearl-white 4Runner and opened the passenger door for me. He hadn't engaged the safety-lock—*confident*—and he hadn't seemed bothered by my attentiveness. I'd looked over my shoulder. Stared at streetlights, signs, landmarks, and intersections.

Jackson Monroe lived six blocks away from me.

How close he'd been, how long he'd watched, how easily he could've cut my throat. But instead, he'd stalked, learned, waited. Like a leopard, or an anaconda, or a wolf.

"Adrian," he said, pulling me out of my thoughts.

I blinked, turning my face upward, toward him. "Yeah?"

The evening sharpened his slender nose and scarred mouth. "Are you thirsty?"

"I could drink." I needed a drink.

He dusted his hand along my lower back and walked to the sleek bar, constructed of live-edge wood, and brought back two flutes of bubbly amber liquid. "Have you ever tried mead?"

Once, at a renaissance fair. I took the glass. "No."

"Wine made with honey. This one is infused with cherries and cinnamon."

I took a sip and glanced around the strange, repurposed space. The welcome area where a finely dressed host had checked us in was stationed just outside the woodshop. Guests cozied up to grazing stations stocked with appetizers and puckered their lips after each sip of mead, wine, or champagne. I had nothing in common with any of them. Designer bags dangled from delicate elbows. Teeth—bought in Thailand, or Mexico, or Israel—glimmered too white under the bohemian mason jar lighting. Conversation ebbed and flowed. Politics, investment ventures, vacations, Wall Street.

"What're we doing here, Jackson." I framed the question as a statement. I felt faint for a moment, realizing I'd said *we* rather than *you*. "I know legal assistants earn above a living wage, but do you have anything in common with..." I finished my mead. "...people like this?"

Jackson, dapper and tall, held his glass between two knuckles and huffed out a laugh. "What? You think a broke bitch like me can't afford a nice dinner?"

"That's not what I said."

"I choose my outings wisely. Why?"

"You like nice things. That's all."

"Explain."

I shrugged, plucking at the middle button on my coat. "My clothes. Your clothes. Your kitchenware." I rolled my eyes. "Your apartment,"

I deadpanned, and shot him a cold glance. "Your car. You either have money or you found money."

"And if it's both?"

"Then it's both."

Jackson stepped behind me. I stilled. Kept my eyes straight ahead as he followed my bicep to my forearm, skirting his hand along my wrist to dislodge the empty flute from my hold. His lips met my ear, featherlight, intentionally gentle.

"And if I told you I live-streamed the decapitation of the last person I cooked?" His tongue clicked on the last word. "If I told you a handful of infatuated viewers with deep pockets and untapped curiosity paid to watch me remove her heart..." He hummed, running the tip of his nose along my hairline. "What then, Adrian? Would that explain my impressive financial prowess? Or should I tell you I have an OnlyFans? Which do you prefer?"

My pulse doubled. I heard the blood in my veins, rushing fast, *faster*. I fought against a bout of dizziness and cleared my throat. I should've been afraid. I *wanted* to be afraid. A part of me might've been, but I hardly felt it. Everything was slick and heady in my skull as if someone had cracked me open and coated my amygdala in motor oil. My limbic system misfired. Flight, fight, freeze deconstructed itself into something new. I blinked. Swallowed. Replayed what he'd said to me—slowly, quickly—and told my lungs to keep functioning, my knees to stay locked, my back to remain straight.

Trust is a precious, finite thing, I thought.

Jackson visited the bar and returned with two more glasses. He hummed expectantly, waiting for an answer.

"Why do you do it?" I asked.

"You didn't answer my ques—"

"Answer mine first." I took the flute and rolled the edge of the glass against my bottom lip.

"Because I can," he said. His earthy eyes narrowed playfully, and he put his thumb to the corner of my mouth, swiping away a splatter of mead. "Because I did it once, then twice, and decided I shouldn't stop."

"Why not?"

"Because I like it," he said, and sucked the wine from his digit. I remembered my blood on his thumb, too. How he'd brought the redness to his mouth and tasted me while our dinner simmered on the stove. "Because it suits me."

"Yet you want to die?" I challenged.

"Everyone dies," he snapped. He took a long pull from his drink. "Your turn. Answer me, Adrian. Do you want the truth or a lie?"

I turned the question over in my mind. I thought *lie*, because yes, a lie, a consumable thing, an answer to my prayers, a bit of normalcy to chew on, swallow, regurgitate. *Lie to me*, I wanted to say. *Pull the wool over my eyes, make me believe in beautiful falsehoods, allow me the pleasure of ignorance.* But I followed the curved exterior on the half-full flute and said, "The truth."

Because I never had. Because I was in a lawless, inescapable place with a dangerous, captivating man.

I could've found the strength to hate myself, could've excavated it like a well-hidden curse, but I didn't.

I wanted to run, I wanted to stay, I wanted to vomit, I wanted to kiss him, I wanted to impale myself on a rusty wood saw, I wanted to pluck my own eyes out, I wanted to pulverize his flesh like orange pulp, I wanted to undo all he'd done to me. I wanted to be who I'd been before he took me. I wanted to know who I had the capability to become in the role of his consequence, his judgment. I wanted everything and nothing. I wanted to live, I wanted to die.

"You're purgatory," I said, so suddenly it sent a shiver down my spine.

Jackson's brows twitched together. He smiled, barely. "Excuse me?"

"I'm your judgment. You're my purgatory."

Before he could respond, the host who'd greeted us stepped in front of the rustic entryway separating the welcome area from the refined woodshop. "Guests, if you'd please follow me this way." He swept his arm toward an array of candlelit tables assembled with cushioned chairs and place settings. "Each table is labeled, the mead, wine, or champagne you chose during your booking is waiting for you, and the first course will be served momentarily."

Jackson took my hand. "Judgement," he echoed under his breath, exhaling. Relieved, almost.

"I could still surprise you," I assured.

He pulled my chair out for me. "I don't doubt that."

A server swooped by to deliver two frosty water glasses and pour us each sparkling Rhodomel mead. A violinist played sultry, howling music, breaking up the conversational chatter echoing through the almost empty factory, and the candlelight dancing across Jackson's face carved him into a ghost. Gold hollowed all the deepest places—cheekbones, upper labret, temples, eye sockets—and accentuated his big hands, folded on the table, and the black moon tattooed on his middle finger. He was gilded and sophisticated, and I didn't bother forcing my eyes elsewhere as we both sipped our mead.

It was silent in the way all comfortable and uncomfortable things were silent. He watched me; I watched him. He unlaced his hands and dragged his finger along a dent in the tablecloth; I followed the movement like a hawk freshly tossed from the nest. There was simplicity in it. How complication and terror eased into forced comfortability and intrigue.

If he'd manipulated me, he'd done a wonderful job. But I knew better.

Jackson was testing me. Pressing against my resolve, treating it like a bruise. Waiting for me to flinch.

"Did you like the taste of me?" he asked.

I kept my back straight, my posture poised and elegant. "I did. Did you enjoy the show?"

"Yeah," he rasped, grinning. "Will you try to kill me again, Adrian?"

"Probably," I said. Truth for truth. Secret for secret. "Do you believe in God?"

"I am God. Do you believe in Darwinism?"

"I do." I paused. Slid the thought around in my mouth until it solidified. "Do you intend to break me?"

"How so?"

"Make me like you."

"You're already like me," he said, and winked.

The first course arrived, carried by two servers, and was placed in front of us at the exact same time. Brie bubbled in personal-sized cast-iron skillets, paired with sliced apples, brown bread, and a fruit compote.

I spread hot cheese onto a piece of fluffy bread. "How do you know?"

"Intuition."

Jackson ate quietly. He spread jam and cheese on bread, same as I did, and hummed pleasantly when an apple slice crunched under his teeth. The conversation came and went. At one point, he asked me if I liked the food. I said *yes*, and it was true. We talked about music, film, religion, and church. When I told him I believed God had a plan for me, he smiled like a jackal, and when Jackson told me he'd murdered his first love, I dipped my finger into the skillet and collected an impolite glob of cheese.

"Why?" I asked.

The next course was roasted pheasant, vegetables, and risotto. Rosemary and juniper berries perfumed the air.

"I wanted to keep her," he said, tenderly, as if he'd opened an old letter. "I wanted to have her in every single way I could possibly have her. Consume her, become her. When I realized she was afraid of me, I knew there was no undoing what I'd done. I couldn't uninstall her fear, so I removed her from it."

It was as if I'd stepped into a fever dream. I felt entirely awake, but everything was hazy and bright, like I'd smoked a joint or taken a pill. My skin grew tighter. My heart, heavier. The thrill, adrenaline, terror, fascination latched onto my nervous system. It suckled there, an obsessive compulsion I couldn't shake.

Again, we ate. And we talked. Jackson asked if I'd thought about murder, and I said *yes*, because every person did, sometimes. I thought of my hair in his closet, and being tangled in his bedding, and my saliva on his sheets, and asked if he ever thought about getting caught. *Everyone gets caught*, he said, laughing through it, and touched the toe of his shoe to my shin beneath the table. I told him I wasn't a good dancer, and he refused to believe me. He told me he enjoyed gardening, and I refused to believe him. I smiled, somehow. And I laughed, and I ate, and I drank, and I thought *this feels too unreal, this feels too natural, this feels too ordinary*. I told myself to remember the word *abducted*, to sear it into my grey matter, and then I told myself to forget how he'd looked at me last night.

More mead. Another dish—pan-seared elk, crispy purple potatoes, mushroom gravy—and dessert after that—clementine custard with cream, served with coffee.

"What do you fantasize about?" Jackson dragged the silver dessert spoon between his lips, scraping away orange-colored custard. "Be honest."

"What do you mean?" I knew exactly what he meant.

"What's your kink."

Heat bloomed in my face. The alcohol loosened my tongue. Gave me schoolgirl courage. "Consensual non-consent," I said, casually. "The fight, I think. People are typically careful with me, and I wish they weren't. Like, it's a cunt, not a bomb, you know?" I tried to laugh, but it sounded sad. Distant. "I like to be treated with *care*, obviously. I just wish people trusted me to know what I want."

"And what *do* you want, Adrian?"

I licked my lips. "Passion," I confessed.

Jackson gave a slow, thoughtful nod. His eyes were cinders, burning through me, and I couldn't look away from him. We stayed like that, staring at each other, listening to the violinist finish his last song. Our fellow diners applauded for Chef Lucas Soto. I tipped my glass, draining the remaining sip or so of my mead, and desperately tried to rationalize with myself.

God has a plan clashed with *he's enchanting*, tumbled alongside *I want to go home*, and broke apart beside *what's happening to me?*

I did not recognize myself. *Caterpillars never recognize themselves when they begin to evolve.* I did not trust myself. *Does a butterfly trust its wings, or does it listen to instinct?*

"What do you fantasize about, Jackson?"

He lifted his chin. His mouth curved. "Being trusted despite what I am. I don't get off on fear, believe it or not. I never have."

"What *do* you get off on?" I asked.

Everything on the surface of my being was red, blistering, suffocating, and everything beneath the very surface of my skin glowed, nuclear.

"The chase," he said, and his lips split for a grin. "I'm a sucker for desire. Wanting, being wanted."

"I find it hard to believe you'd have trouble in that department."

Jackson blinked. Surprise crossed his face, electric and genuine. "Explain."

"Confidence." I shrugged. "It's sexy."

"I think my confidence is often mistaken for something else."

"Like?"

"A threat, I guess."

"Then it wouldn't be a mistake, would it?"

The dining experience ended. Guests rose from their seats, smoothed their couture, and made for the makeshift parking lot. All the while, Jackson analyzed me, studying my face with quick flicks of his lashes. He looked handsome in that empty room, flanked by abandoned tables, set ablaze by a weak, half-melted candle. I wished I could've seen what he saw. I wanted to know if I'd stoked a yearning in him, the same way he'd caused something fiery and wild to ignite inside me.

I wanted to pluck him open. Unstitch his practiced guise.

I wanted to know if I had any control at all.

But his eyes, how they roamed, told me I had *something* he couldn't particularly resist. A kind of power, maybe. A dose of misguided grace.

"You're fascinating," he said, and stood, offering me his hand. "Your place next, right?"

I hadn't forgotten, but the reality struck me like a fist.

I let out a breath, sharp and poignant, and nodded. "Yeah, yes. Please."

An eternity came and went.

I fidgeted, pulling at the webbing between my fingers in the passenger seat while Jackson turned the wheel, parking alongside the curb across the street from my apartment building. I didn't live in a nice area, or a bad area. It was cheap, and halfway decent, and suited for people who were street-smart. People who had been poor once, and maybe still were. Runaways. Waitresses, hospitality workers, teachers, starving artists. Some of the apartments were well-kept and modern. Others hardly furnished and mostly empty. I didn't know my neighbors. No one really looked at each other unless we were crossing paths on the staircase or unlocking our doors in the same hall on a quiet night.

No one probably realized I'd been gone.

The fire escape on the building next door to mine faced my living room window. I pictured Jackson there, dressed in black from head to toe, arm propped on his bent knee, watching me amble around in my underwear, reading, working, eating, praying.

"Do you stalk all your victims like you stalked me?" I asked.

Jackson pulled the key from the ignition. Silence stretched. "No. Why?"

"How do you choose?"

He hummed dismissively. "If I'm cooking them, I'm picky. The first time was a fluke—I was lovesick. But the second time, I found someone upscale. Green juice slurping, yoga practicing, Tesla driving piece of shit," he whispered, fondly. "It's like buying organic, you know." He faced me, shrugging one shoulder. "You pay a high price for grass-fed. I wanted the best, so I found someone who treated their body like a fuckin' temple. But if I'm not having them for dinner, well, I just..." He scrunched his nose. "...follow my heart, I guess."

Follow your heart. I mouthed the words, repeating them silently. "And your heart led you to me?"

Jackson narrowed his eyes. When he smiled, I felt the same way a doe would on the hollow end of a loaded rifle. "Go get your things." He fished in his pocket, tossed my keychain into my lap, and unlocked the passenger door. *He unlocked the door.* "I'll see you in a minute."

I resisted running. The streetlamp on the corner flickered. I told my legs to stay steady, *one foot in front of the other, yes, go*, and willed the tremble in my hand to subside as I grasped the front door. The polished shoes Jackson had given me clicked on the linoleum in the lobby. The elevator was still out of order, striped with caution tape and blocked by an orange cone. I touched the ugly bronze mailboxes on my way to the staircase. Once I turned the corner and entered the claustrophobic stairwell, I ran. My thighs burned. I heaved in breath after breath, scrambling on the banister, pulling myself closer to the fifth floor.

I shouldered through the door. Tripped over a welcome mat. Righted myself and kept running. I angled my key toward the lock-slot. Missed. Grasped my wrist, steadied myself, and tried again. Once the lock slid free, I stepped inside—cold, I'd left a window open—and slammed the door—twisted the lock, hit the lightswitch—whirled around, frantically glancing at the couch, television, coffee table, galley kitchen, unmade bed. Everything was how I'd left it, how it'd always been.

What now?

The curtain twisted, tossed by a shy breeze. I'd left underwear puddled on the bathroom floor. A dish in the sink. A pizza box yawned open on the table. Most people wouldn't cry over a shitty studio apartment, but I did. I walked into the bathroom, grabbed my lotion, and slathered my arms in a familiar scent. I didn't sob or anything. I cried like someone would at the end of a good movie, or at an opera, or when they heard their favorite song.

I brushed my teeth with my own toothbrush. Dabbed my own balm on my lips. Raked my fingers through my hair, and exhaled a sigh of relief, and felt everything, all at once, drop out from under my feet. I knew that sound—the metal *glide, shimmy, snap* of a key in the lock—and I ran. I wish I knew why. I wish I could've refined myself in that moment. Became more. Better. But adrenaline seeped through every inch of me, and I couldn't parse any of the passing panic.

I smacked the light switch, darkening the small space, and opened the cutlery drawer, snatching a wide-mouthed knife by the handle.

Jackson Monroe entered my apartment. "Adrian," he said, sighing my name.

I lunged. I wasn't strong, I knew that, but I shoved the blade beneath his chin and slammed myself against him, trapping Jackson against the door.

"You made a copy of my fucking key," I seethed.

He craned his neck, lifting his chin away from the knife. "Easy, little dove."

"What is this, huh? You take me to a fancy fucking dinner, tell me about your first love, talk to me about *killing* people, and then follow me up here to, what, to... to..." I swallowed hard. Blushed furiously. I pushed the knife against his neck and watched his Adam's apple leap. "Stop playing games."

"You think I wouldn't make a key to your studio? You read my journal; you've seen inside my head. At least be honest with yourself. You knew I had a key. You knew what I'd do." His hand graced my hip, fingertips sneaking beneath my shirt. "You want the fight; I want the chase. We both win."

I chewed my bottom lip. My skin clung to my bones. Everything was too close, too visceral, too right there.

"Say no," Jackson whispered. He pushed his index finger into my waistband and tugged, sliding his digit along the top of my pants. "And mean it."

"I could cut your throat."

"You could."

"I..." I felt blanched. Dunked, boiled, left to burn. "Why'd you kiss me earlier?"

"Because you wanted me to."

I scraped the knife upward, setting it in the dent just beneath his chin. "Bold assumption."

Jackson shifted his hand away from my waist and pushed the knife away with two fingers. The tip scraped fine stubble on his chin, invisible to the naked eye. "Say no," he said again, and leaned into me, molding his body to mine, guiding me backward. "*And mean it.*"

When he grasped my wrist and squeezed, I struggled. And when he bent my arm backward, I cried out and dropped the knife, resisting his strength until I stumbled.

I thrashed out of his grip and stepped away from him. Noticed how he tracked me, following every move I made, and resisted the urge to shout when he surged toward me. Adrenaline soaked through every bone, every ligament, every fiber of me. I swatted as he grappled for my midsection. Swung my elbow, missed, tripped and kicked, landed a blow with my foot to his thigh. He grunted, huffed, and pushed me. Sent me into the wall next to the window.

Before I could right myself, Jackson was there again, taking both my forearms and slamming my hands above my head.

I'd dreamed about things like this. Monsters holding me captive in the night. Many-winged angels with lion eyes and scorpion tails bending me to their will.

He breathed hard. I did, too. We stayed like that, Jackson's palms pressed to my pulse, my breath coming in urgent puffs.

"Do you want me?" Jackson asked.

"No," I said, breathless. The lie was easy, predetermined.

He slid his hands higher, curling his fingers over my clenched fists. "Will you scream for me?"

"*No.*"

He leaned closer, angling his mouth toward my ear. "Are you scared, Adrian?"

I was. I wasn't. A thousand different feelings stampeded through me, all synonymous with desire, all cousins of fear. Distressed, dismayed, horrified, *aching*.

I turned my face toward him, a subconscious reflex, and searched for his lips. He didn't make me wait. Didn't make me work for it. When Jackson kissed me, it was all consuming. His mouth seared mine. Teeth snagged my lip and damp breath coasted into my throat. I fell into him. Alice, rabbits, potions—everything. I fell, and I spun, and I knew I wouldn't be able to claw my way out. It'd taken a mere few days for him to unscrew the control I had over myself. Jackson Monroe was the drug I'd been taught to stay away from. The powder at the party you avoided. The liquor that caused blackouts.

But I moaned between his parted lips and when he released my hands, I grabbed his face, kept him close, and traced his molars with my tongue. I saw myself hitting the pavement again. All those daydreams I'd had. The commitment I hadn't made to a death that never came. Jackson grasped beneath my backside and lifted me, coaxing my thighs to curl around his waist. I inhaled raggedly and met his gaze through half-lidded eyes. I imagined him covered in blood. I thought of his meals. How kidneys came apart between his teeth. The way a trachea might crack when he closed his jaws around it.

Jackson picked me up. I hated my size—small, delicate—but I still didn't expect him to have the strength to toss me onto the bed. I landed gracelessly on the quilted comforter. He mapped my torso. My shirt pooled in the bend at each of his thumbs and his fingers skirted my stomach, chest, shoulders until the garment was tossed away. Being undressed by him was nothing like being bare beneath him last night. His deft touch and the firm press of his hand beneath my belly button opened a pit inside me. I was suddenly ravenous. Delirious. Unkempt. The immediacy of my own lust shot through me like an arrow.

"What do you want?" Jackson went to his knees at my bedside.

I couldn't fathom it. Couldn't make my mouth shape the words.

He unfastened my belt and pulled my pants away, sliding them down my legs and onto the floor. "Adrian."

"What the fuck does anyone in this situation *want*, Jackson?" I snapped, covering my face with my hands. "I want you to..."

"To?" He traced my cunt through my underwear.

"Pretend you want me," I choked out. "Make it last. Give me something to remember." *Something to take with me.* "Something to apologize for when I stand before God."

Jackson opened his mouth over my underwear. His tongue pressed against the fabric, and I keened, flexing my hips toward him. I wanted him to devour me.

"Why would I pretend?" he asked, nuzzling my thigh. "When the Red Sea split did the world look away?"

I shook my head.

"You're my forbidden fruit." Another open kiss. Cotton, soaked. "Dangling there, unused to being eaten."

I'm not pure. I held my tongue. "What do *you* want?"

Jackson yanked my underwear away and covered my cock with his mouth, suckling wetly at pinkened flesh. A noise tore itself from my throat. I expected teeth. Harsh pleasure, the kind scripted in bad porn. I thought being with him might hurt, but the pleasure he offered was fierce and overwhelming. He tongued at the sensitive area beneath my small cock. Plunged inside me. Lapped firmly at my cunt, stroke after stroke, until my spine bent and I was coming, hard and fast, with my hands fisted in the quilt and my jaw slackened.

I hadn't experienced it before—coming like that, so quickly, with someone new.

I grabbed at the blanket, then reached for him, securing one hand on the back of his head and the other on his forearm. He kept my legs spread, gripping the back of my thighs, and circled my cock with his tongue. My hips lurched and I reared off the bed, curling toward him. Heat and pleasure blinded me. I gasped and shook. Boyish sounds and pathetic mewls punched out of me, clipped and pitchy.

I was in my home—*my home*—with the man who had taken me.

I was in my bed—*my bed*—with the killer who had abducted me.

Nothing about it felt right, or safe, or fair. But it felt worthy. Believable in a sick way.

I could've put the pocket knife through his windpipe last night. I could've opened his throat minutes ago.

But I was gasping, panting, watching him rise to his feet and strip away his clothes. I was drenched, shaken, taken off guard, open-mouthed and eager. Shadow clung to his bare shoulders. His cock arced toward his inked stomach, flushed and entirely normal. He took himself in his hand and stroked, staring at the quivering mess he'd left of me, shrouded in darkness, silhouetted by everything I held near and dear. The things I'd worked for. My life was all packed in a tiny square. His thumb pushed, following the curve of his cock.

"Say no," he whispered.

I was drunk on pleasure. "No," I said, peeling my tongue off the roof of my mouth. "Don't fucking touch me."

"Mean it."

"Make me," I bit.

Jackson craned over the bed and latched his hand around my throat.

I thrashed. "Let me go." I didn't want him to. I wanted to go limp. But the thrill, the excitement, the high that came with being completely, utterly out of control was intoxicating. I kicked my feet. "Let me go," I whimpered, swatting, clawing. "Jackson, please." I was begging *for* him. "Enough, just... Please, just..."

Brown eyes narrowed. A coy smile tugged at his lips. "Are you asking for mercy, Adrian?"

I set my teeth. "C'mon," I whispered. The game was over. Just like that, my body and brain chemistry separated, oil and water. My tone changed. Grew gruffer, angrier. "Get off."

"Done already?"

"If you don't want—"

"Don't tell me you're that easy to fool," Jackson said. He relaxed his hold on my throat, but kept me pinned, looming over me.

I stopped fighting. Stopped playing along. Stopped moving altogether. I let my weight sink into the bed and placed my hand atop his, tracing the knuckles clamped around my neck.

"I don't like to be teased," I mumbled, and it was the sad truth. I was far too self-conscious for it. "I like to be sure of things."

Jackson's expression softened. Had he ever looked at another victim the same way? Tenderly. "Do you need me to tell you?"

"I need you to show me," I said. If I was going to die, I would die after having him. If I was already dead, I would spend the afterlife like that, poised beneath him, asking for passion. I dug my fingernails into the top of his hand. "Show me," I murmured. "Show me, show me—"

Jackson squeezed until I could no longer speak then pried at my mouth with his own. He allowed me to breathe only when he finally exhaled, filling my lungs with what he'd gathered, held, warmed. I was tired already, worn out from an explosive orgasm, but I kissed him long and deep and gave no resistance when he bent my knees over his forearms and rested my legs in the crook of his elbows.

We fucked like old gods. I imagined it was how artists captured sex in paintings and sculptures. His body sinking into mine, my hands on his shoulders, running along the sides of his neck, finding purchase on places where his skin was thin and vulnerable. I touched the scab above his clavicles. Held onto him as his forehead bumped mine, and our noses tapped, and his breath ghosted my cheek. His cock widened me. His hips knocked against my own, and I rose to meet him, urging him deeper. When he put his teeth to my neck, I closed my eyes and clutched to him, searching his shoulder blades for a place my nails could bite.

I'd never had a man show me his pleasure. Lovemaking had always been silent, awkward. But Jackson made encouraging noises, moaning beneath my ear, chewing at my flesh, worrying a bruise there. I thought he might draw blood. Thought he might tear me open. A part of me hoped he would.

When Jackson snapped his hips harder, faster, I panted and relaxed, giving myself over to him. To be used, to be had. Pleasure climbed from my groin into my abdomen and spread like ichor. It was a slow orgasm, pulsing through me, tightening my muscles, causing me to shake and whine. It lingered. Tortured me, really. My eyes were unfocused, stomach clenched, toes curled, and I thought it wouldn't end, wouldn't let up.

Jackson sank his teeth into me when he came. The core of me was hot. Coated in him. I felt soaked. I was so slick he slipped out and glided along my swollen cock. He rutted against my hip, shaft skipping across my messy cunt until his movement slowed, and his jaw loosened, and his breathing dimmed.

I didn't expect him to reach between us and fill me again. I didn't expect him to kiss me again, either.

But he stayed impossibly close, sheathed by my spent body, and licked into my mouth.

I was trapped in it, this lust he'd instilled in me. When he finally pulled out and turned me onto my stomach, I went. And when he spread wetness from my cunt to my ass, I didn't protest. He held me by my nape and fucked my backhole, grunting, sighing, cooing at me. *Gorgeous*, he whispered through gritted teeth, but I hardly heard him. I stared at my darkened studio, eyes unfocused, vision fuzzy, and kept my knees spread, enduring the pleasant burn, the unnatural pain of his cock jammed inside me. I should've hated him. I should've hollered and knocked him away. But I loved the sting. Craved the careless way he used me, like I was something to claim, like I was worth the effort.

He made a winded noise and spit on my hole. "Do you like that?"

"No," I lied, fisting my hands in the quilt. My cunt leaked.

Jackson fucked me ruthlessly. He slid his hand into my hair, pushed my face against the bed, and I listened to our bodies connect, to the rhythm of our skin meeting, the bed creaking, his breath deepening, audibly rising. Delightful pain radiated in my lower half and my empty pussy spasmed.

Whore found dead in studio apartment. I reminded myself to inhale. *Femboy raped and killed by mystery murderer.*

I couldn't come again, but I wanted to.

"Good boy," Jackson moaned, and pressed in as deep as he could, grinding against my cheeks. "Good fucking boy."

My lashes fluttered. The blanket muffled my moan, but I pushed back against him, encouraging him to grip my nape, and force me down. He didn't spurt inside me—couldn't, probably—but he trembled and gasped, and I knew he'd finished.

I felt drunk or high. I couldn't move, couldn't do anything except breathe and lie there, dirtied, roughened, left to wilt.

The bed dipped. Clothes rustled, laces pulled, a sigh fluttered into the darkness. I expected him to get me dressed, but Jackson kissed my tailbone like a gentleman. His footsteps faded. The front door closed.

Wait, I wanted to say. *Wait, wait.*

The lock clicked, fastened from the other side.

I'm alone. I closed my eyes. Jackson dripped down my thigh. Stained me, permanently. *I'm alone.*

I WAS RETURNED ON a Thursday, and I did not know myself. Not anymore. Not after that.

I woke sore and disoriented. I found my phone on the coffee table the morning after Jackson had shared my bed. The device was fully charged, stacked with Discord notifications, and riddled with text messages. A few unanswered proposals sat in my inbox. I looked for his thumbprint on the glass surface, searched for any remnant of him other than the blotchy bruise he'd planted on my neck and found nothing.

Not a shred of him on my iPhone.

No trace of him in my studio.

A day went by. I answered everyone who'd reached out. Told the group chat I was fine. Sent my resume to a few interested parties.

A second day came and went.

I paced. Cried. Pulled back the curtain and scanned the sidewalk, looking for a man who never appeared. *Had it happened?* I went to my reflection for comfort. The hickey was still there. His teeth, little half-moons, imprinted on me. *Yes, of course it'd happened*. I remembered his mouth on mine. How I'd excavated a lost piece of myself from deep within him, like a vulture picked marrow from a corpse. I hardly slept; hardly ate.

On the third day, I left my apartment. I went to the café across the street, ordered a vanilla latte with oatmilk, extra hot, and wondered if Jackson was watching from some hidden place. I pretended to work at an empty table. Searched his name—Jackson Monroe—on Facebook, and Twitter, and every other God-forsaken social media platform. I looked for police reports, arrest records, the law firm he might work for, and came away with nothing. *Is it a fake name?* I felt faint, so I bought a scone and nibbled at its round, maple-flavored corner. *Why wouldn't it be?* I shut my laptop. Opened it again. Chewed my nail, finished my pastry, and went back to my apartment. I scolded myself for hoping he'd be there, standing in the center of my studio, waiting for me. But he wasn't.

How had a mere three days rewired my consciousness? I should've gone to the police. I should've given a detailed description of him to an investigator. I should've retraced my steps, and shown the authorities to his apartment, and made sure he could never hurt anyone ever again.

I missed his cooking, though. And the way his focus sharpened while he was inside me. How his blood coated my tongue like expensive wine.

The thought made me pause as I brushed my teeth and got ready for bed. *Communion*. I stared at my naked reflection. *Confession*. I chewed on my toothbrush, pushing bristles into the crevice between bone and gum. *Right, yes.* I nodded at myself. *Yes, good, okay.*

On Sunday, I went to church. I sat in the third pew on the left side and listened to Father Hudson preach about temptation. It was a fitting sermon, quoting passages from Genesis, Leviticus, and Corinthians. People around me nodded and clapped. Prayed silently. Said *amen*. I knelt, tapped two fingers against my forehead, shoulders, sternum, and opened my mouth for unleavened bread. I imagined Jackson's split flesh as Father Hudson tipped the chalice against my lips. Apologized to God when the daydream wouldn't fade and took shelter in the red-draped confessional after the service had concluded.

"May God be with you," Father Hudson said. I saw the rosary twined around his conjoined wrinkly hands through the grate in the divider between the booths.

"And also with you, Father." I didn't have the courage to search for whatever microphone—recording device, *something*—Jackson had hidden between the wood slats or velvet upholstery, but I hoped it was still there. I wanted him to hear me. "Forgive me, but my repentance is complicated today. I feel as though I shouldn't be here. Like I should be thanking God rather than questioning the path he's set for me."

"Go on."

"I met a man." My tongue pressed against the back of my teeth. I closed my eyes. "A terrible man. He's the definition of wrong for me, so to speak. I'm... I should be *glad* to be away from him, you know? I should be rejoicing, honestly. But I..." It was as if he'd crawled inside me. "I feel like he's a compound fracture, busting through my skin. I want to dress the wound, but I'm not brave enough to put the bone back where it belongs. I want to move on, but I find myself overwhelmed with the urge to be near him." I imagined myself as Jackson's skin, tucked against vitality. Organ, ligament, nerves. "I should want him to stay away from me, but I want him to find me again." I wanted to put my hand in his mouth. I wanted to eat the tattoo on his stomach. "Is this part of his holy plan, Father? Should I be afraid?"

The priest was quiet for a long time. "Do you fear you're being tested?"

"Yes," I said, relieved, exasperated. "And I don't think I'm strong enough to resist."

"Resist what, exactly?"

Jackson. Myself. What we could be together. What we would do. "The irresponsible urge to satisfy my hedonistic impulses. Tell me how to steel myself against it." Against him. "Tell me what to do."

"Only God can guide you." Suspicion filled Father Hudson's voice. "Are you all right, Adrian? You're safe here. What you say in this confessional is between you and the holy spirit. I only serve as its vessel."

I stared at the plain, brown crucifix nailed to the divider beside my head. "Have you ever been scared of your destiny, Father?"

"My destiny was decided for me," he said, so simply.

Right, I mouthed, and sighed. "Do you believe in false prophets? Or in false gods?"

"That's an unusual question."

"I believe one found me," I said. *Took me.* "I think I've been poached."

"The Lord is faithful. He will guard you against evil. Thessalonians." Father Hudson shifted. The bench creaked. "Find solace in prayer, Adrian. Hold fast to your faith and comfort yourself with an act of contrition. Be blessed, son of Christ, for you are made new." The priest paused for a moment and cleared his throat, leveling his voice to sound more human, more accessible. "You're always welcome here. If you need to talk or... Or find shelter. The church is always open, night or day."

"Thank you, Father." I opened the door and stepped out, striding quickly toward the door.

The Virgin Mary stood before the entrance of the church, palms open, ushering lost souls into the sanctuary. I could hardly look at her as I left. Could barely think clearly, or see straight, or get a handle on my mind.

Did you hear me, Jackson?

A car horn blared. Strangers crossed at the intersection. Sundown painted the sky pink and orange, and Aurora blushed before nightfall.

I looked for him in windows. Searched for the crescent moon on his knuckle, and the fine structure of his face, and the scar on his mouth, and thought of unstitching my skin and fastening it to his skeleton. What it might be like to swallow his heart. How it might feel to be pulverized, juiced; digested. I thought of everything that made me afraid, and everything that thrilled me.

I prayed, too. Begged my sin to whisper. *Don't listen, Holy Father, don't listen.*

Abandonment sank between my vertebrae. The spinal-tap *pop* of Jackson's presence fit inside me like a hollow needle. I dreamed of him. I searched for him. The time I'd spent dwelling on escape in his apartment, on rescue and freedom, morphed into reprehensible mania. I lost track of time. Hours became days. It wasn't until I realized I needed to take my next T-dose that I calculated the time I'd been away from him.

A week. An eternity.

I cleaned my studio. Moved the bed. Adjusted the nightstand. Arranged my closet and re-folded the clothes in my dresser. When there was nothing left to shift or change, I dressed in denim pants and a thin, oversized sweater, and walked into the night.

Streetlamps flickered. Every long, slender shadow stole my attention. I glanced down darkened alleys. Turned my gaze toward the rooftops. Scanned the empty, chilly city for someone deadly lurking close by. I walked to the bar where I'd been taken. The grimy tables and empty bartop at Corkscrew were the same as always. A few regulars sipped pints and watched football, and Bradley cleaned glasses with a rag. Excitement used to ring inside me at the sight of him. He was entirely normal. Tall, sort of muscular, blessed with a standardly handsome face. He wore his hair long, tired back into a ponytail, and sometimes groomed the wiry blond hair on his cheeks and chin.

"Hey," he said, like always.

I forced a smile and sat at the bar. He poured my usual before I had the chance to ask for it. Whiskey, neat.

"Haven't seen you in a while."

"Been busy," I said. I shot the drink back and tapped the empty glass.

Bradley poured another. "Sticking around for a minute?"

"I don't have anywhere else to be."

I nursed my second drink. Bradley moved around the bar with ease, serving drinks and passing baskets of buffalo wings through the kitchen window. Cheap lighting kept the room dim. Insects and rodents made cities in the walls and under the floor, chewing tiny holes through the wood. I focused on the stained green expanse of an empty pool table. The felt was splotchy. Torn at the corners. I thought about Jackson, holding a stick, wearing a baseball cap to shield his face, watching me flirt with Bradley like a doe-eyed fool. He'd probably seen me set my elbow on the bar, cradle my chin, and grin expectantly. Followed me with his eyes as I trailed Bradley into the bathroom or laughed at one of his poorly told jokes. All for a little bit of recognition. The chance of being touched in a way that left me somewhere outside of starving. Not satisfied, not ravenous, but mildly satiated.

"I'm off soon," Bradley said.

I blinked away from the pool table and nodded. "Plans?"

"Yeah, I mean, sort of. We can smoke, though."

Bradley probably had a girlfriend or a wife. Smoke always meant *share a joint, suck my dick, ride me*. I'd never fucked him at his house, never seen him outside of the bar, never been asked on a date. It was always bathroom stalls, or alleyways, or backseats. Sometimes he made me come. Most of the time, he didn't.

But I craved being touched. Having someone on me. Being wanted.

I tried to picture Jackson where Bradley stood. Used my imagination to piece together Jackson's scarred smile, broad shoulders, trim waist. Even as I followed Bradley through the back door and walked into the foggy night, I attempted to materialize Jackson over top of him. Fine, dark clothing. The ink on his belly. How his thumb jutted from his palm, knife-like.

"So, where've you been?" Bradley asked. He didn't turn to look at me as he spoke. Just crossed the parking lot, beelining for his car.

"Around," I said.

Movement, like a bat or a raccoon, darted by in the corner of my eye. Too big to be a critter, though. Fast, premeditated movement. Like a shark after a seal; like a puma launching from a branch. My brain registered the blur too late, but my heart *knew*. The paranoid, unhinged part of me that hadn't stopped thinking of him or waiting for him recognized Jackson Monroe, even in the pitch, even in absolute darkness.

I didn't call Bradley's name—I should've—and I didn't try to block the killing blow—I should've—and I didn't move when the blade, black as night, opened Bradley's throat. One moment, Bradley had turned around to smile at me, and the next, a gloved hand snuck around his face, covered his mouth, and blood—hot, irony—splattered my face.

Hearing someone die was an unusual thing. The gurgle, choke. Bradley stared, bewildered, like a dog looked after wandering onto a busy road, and his knees buckled. He slumped then crashed, revealing Jackson, swathed in all black. Turtleneck, pants, boots, gloves. A half-face mask covered his nose, mouth, and neck, embroidered with white accents to resemble a skull. He flipped the knife and tilted his head, assessing me like an adversary.

I didn't scream. I didn't run. I didn't sob, or stumble, or gasp.

Bradley's death did nothing to me despite it happening right in front of me. I rolled my lips together. His blood was sticky on my mouth, blooming penny-rich when I swallowed. Liquid dampened my eyebrow. Clumped in my eyelashes. Went cold on my cheek. Nausea came and went, churning, rippling in my core, then fading.

"You…" I was at a loss for words. I wanted to wake up. *Wake up.* "Jackson… I…" It happened all at once. Panic, grief, fear, regret. "*Why?* He didn't—he didn't do anything! What…" I sank both hands into my hair and heaved in deep breaths. *No.* I whimpered, finally allowing my gaze to fall. Bradley bled out. I inched away, dodging the red lake leaking from his sliced flesh. "What the fuck was the point of this? Why him? Why—"

"You were the cruel end of every joke he told to his buddies," Jackson said, shrugging. "Slut, nobody, quick fuck, cheap, easy. *He just keeps comin' back*," he mocked, and sighed through his nose. "*Laziest lay of my life* was something he enjoyed repeating, like a one-trick, flightless parrot."

I gaped. "Yeah, and he didn't have to fucking die for it, Jackson," I seethed, lowering my voice. I realized I wasn't crying. I wasn't shocked, or trembling, or gagging. I was upset he'd involved me so directly. I was angry he'd boldly killed someone in public, at my feet. It was a response to recklessness. *You could've shown up at my studio.* I set my teeth. *You could've found me sooner.* "You left," I spat. So childish. So embarrassing.

"You called," he said.

I whirled around, searching the empty backlot for signs of life. "We need to go."

"I spent weeks casing this property. The bar isn't profitable enough to pay for security cameras."

I inched away and finally tiptoed around Bradley's body. *Be upset.* I tried to channel an appropriate response. *Wail, cry, care.* But my mind latched onto Jackson Monroe, standing before me, holding a bloodied knife, and Bradley became insignificant. His existence was a casual blip on the boring expanse of my little life. Two weeks ago, he'd been a habit. Now, he was an inconvenience.

I believed everything Jackson had mentioned. Yeah, Bradley probably joked about me. Yeah, I was nothing to him. I'd curated our experiences together to be exactly that. *Nothing*.

"What now?" I asked.

Jackson tipped his head, curious. "Gross, Adrian. I don't eat garbage."

I scoffed. "Please. I'm talking about the goddamn *mess*, Jackson."

"Leave it. Treat it like roadkill."

"You're serious?"

He pulled down his mask and grinned. "Good to know your only attachment issue is me."

Heat blazed in my chest and cheeks. "You're insufferable. Where's your car?"

"I walked, c'mon."

Strange, how my fear had been stripped. Our relationship was a fresh kill, dressed and hung, empty of what it'd been, ready to become something else entirely. I hardly knew him, yet I felt close to him. I should've seen myself apart from him, but as I kept pace at his side, leaving Bradley's cooling corpse slumped in a small, dark parking lot, I imagined Jackson and I were a new, lonely creature living in two separate bodies.

God had listened, and he'd made up his mind.

After we crossed through the mouth of a nearby alley, Jackson turned. Each movement was calculated. Fluidity was a choice for him.

Everything else, every flick of his wrist, every step and glance, happened with a sureness I'd never known. He put his palm to my chest and eased me backward. My spine met cold concrete. Breath plumed the air. He didn't fumble. Clumsiness was beneath him. When he reached, he found my chin easily, and when he steadied me, I stilled for him.

Jackson opened his mouth and dragged his tongue along my cheek, carefully licking away a splatter of Bradley's blood. I shivered. I cupped his elbow and closed my eyes, surprised to feel cloth on my skin. A handkerchief. Jackson cleaned dutifully, dabbing my temples, wiping my nose. When his lips brushed mine, I welcomed him. Let my jaw relax, enjoyed the unhurried way he kissed the blood from my mouth, and savored the iron flavor passed between us.

"Did he give you passion?" Jackson asked.

I shook my head.

"Then why come out here with him?"

"Are you jealous?"

"Of course."

The ease in which he admitted it—his unrelenting confidence—weakened my knees. "Because I wanted attention."

"From *him?*"

"From anyone."

"Am I anyone, Adrian?"

My ankles weakened. "No," I whispered.

Jackson slipped his hand down the front of my jeans and kissed me again. He touched me over my underwear, teasing with slow, featherlight touches. "If I told you to get on your knees, would you?"

I cracked my eyes open. Everything beneath my belly button boiled. "We need to get out of here—"

"*Would you?*"

I swallowed. "Yes."

His smile broadened. "Get on your knees."

I hesitated. For a moment, I considered smacking him. Running. Screaming for help. But I searched his face instead, settling on the scar striping his curved mouth. "What will you do to me if I don't?" I asked, recalling the small, private dresser tucked away in his closet.

"Leave you," he said, and it was worse than any physical punishment I could imagine.

It was as if he'd sawed open my skull, reached inside, and repurposed the core of me. I felt lobotomized, like a surgery gone wrong, as if he'd punctured the place behind my eye where sympathy and goodness lived and replaced it with a promised future. Something attainable and mistaken. Something glorious and ungodly. I narrowed my eyes and curled my top lip back. When he laughed, I hauled him toward the side of the building and twirled the two of us around, shoving him against the wall.

Jackson's laughter rumbled up and out of him, deeper, more surprised.

I knelt at his feet. The crunchy, damp alleyway soaked through the denim covering my kneecaps, but I hardly noticed. My attention was solely fixed on Jackson's thumb, flicking open his pants, and how effortless he made each movement. The shadows left only the outline of his clothes. Moonlight on his skin was the only evidence he was there at all. When the hot tip of his cock bumped my lips, I took him into my mouth. I never gave finessed blowjobs. Didn't really care to *try*. They weren't pretty—weren't supposed to be. But I sat back on my heels and stared up at Jackson, holding his pinched gaze while I bobbed my head, cradling his shaft with my tongue, gagging only enough to make him grunt. My lips slickened. I watched his chest stutter as I suckled at the tip, tongued at his slit, and only winced when he thrust his hips forward, sliding himself down my throat. I choked. Moaned. Opened my mouth to show him how he looked between my teeth, rutting against my pink tongue, and grinned lazily at the sound he made. Like a curse but lower, growlish and strained.

"Gag," he demanded. "Let me hear it."

I inhaled slowly through my nose and did as he said. I loosened my lips and wiggled my jaw, adjusting myself around his cock, and took him as deep as I could, almost to his root, until my eyes burned, and my throat seized, and I clenched around him. My stomach jumped. My body convulsed. The squelching noise he coaxed out of me was desperate and disgusting. But he came with me like that, coughing on him, trying not to retch on his shoes. Hot, salty come flooded my throat and spackled the roof of my mouth. I gagged again, sending strings of spunk onto my chin. I pushed my thighs together. I was embarrassingly wet.

I milked him until he shied away, leaving my sticky mouth empty. I sucked in a deep breath, filling my achy lungs.

"You're good at that," he said, panting.

I noticed a strangeness in him. A discomfort. He seemed jittery. Off. As if he didn't quite know what to do. I wiped my mouth with the back of my hand. "Sucking dick isn't a skill."

"Get up."

I furrowed my brow. "What's wrong?"

"Like you said, we need to get out of here."

I blinked, taken aback. *Right, yeah.* I glanced sideways, back toward Bradley, and got to my feet.

I tasted blood. Tasted Jackson.

Gingerly, he took my hand. His leather glove felt alien against my palm, but I held on anyway.

Jackson unlocked his apartment. He held the door for me, but I could not move. I stood in the hall, gazing through the open doorway to the place I'd been *kept*. Being invited was a new experience. I imagined him guiding me inside when I'd been drugged and woozy. Remembered clawing at the lock from the inside, and crying in the guest bedroom, and fucking myself in his bed. I scanned the floor. Dragged my gaze to his face. He watched me patiently, toeing off his shoes.

"You don't date, do you," I said, framing the question like a statement. I hadn't meant to speak, but the words snuck out. It was a blatant, blinding thing. An understanding I hadn't come to until right then. I'd miscategorized him. Assumed too much. Jackson could've had whoever he wanted, yes, but he kept himself apart from domesticity for many, many reasons. Obviously. "This is new for you."

"Are you deeming our time together a courtship?" Jackson's brows cinched. His mouth twitched, barely a smile.

"Almost," I said, and urged myself forward.

I entered the familiar cage. The place where I thought I'd die—*might still die*—and removed my shoes.

He closed the door. Locked it. The apartment remained unlit, once again illuminated by moonlight streaming through the slider separating the living room from the balcony. Darkness made for an easier transition. It held us captive, cushioning the dirt and grime that lived beneath Jackson Monroe's polished exterior. Defined who I'd decided to chase. Revealed the person he'd unearthed inside me. Bradley's blood caked uncomfortably in my eyebrow, accidentally skipped by Jackson's gentle cleanse minutes, hours, eons ago. We stood before each other, unmoving, breathing.

"You watched me kill a man," he said. "Someone you knew. Someone you cared for."

I didn't nod. Didn't speak.

He reached for my face but dropped his hand before our flesh met. "Why're you here, Adrian?"

"You associate consequence with death, right? If I'm your consequence, I'm the one who kills you?"

Jackson gave a curt nod.

"But judgment is something different, isn't it? At first, I thought it was confidence, but it was hope, wasn't it? Keeping me here, feeding me whoever you fed me, taking me to dinner, sweet-talking me…" I waited. Watched his expression tighten. "You love me," I blurted, and almost laughed, almost cried. "You stalked me, intending to kill me, but you—"

"Careful, little dove."

"You wanted me to be like you so, *so* badly, but you weren't sure—"

"I was very sure."

"So, you took me. Because you don't know how to be fucking *normal* about—"

"Adrian," he warned, calmly.

"You love me," I said, harsh, whispered.

"Says the man who cried for me in a confessional." He tipped closer, exhaling against my mouth. "Obsession isn't love."

"Yes, it is. For us, it is."

"Us," he echoed. "There's an *us* now?"

"One day, I'll kill you, Jackson. Don't worry."

"I know," he said, softly, like a child.

"But not today."

Jackson pulled his mask off and let it drop. He raked his fingers through his mussed hair and took my hand, guiding me past the kitchen, down the hall, and into his bedroom. It smelled the same, like his cologne, like old books, like peroxide. I followed him into the attached bathroom. Again, we shared the darkness. He undressed me tactfully. It wasn't filled with the rush of new romance or crackling with hushed laughter. We were silent, moving fluidly, plucking at zippers and buttons, tugging at cotton and denim. It was as if I'd known him for a decade. Like we'd met in a past life.

I wanted to eat his heart. I wanted to see inside him—highways of veins, polished organs, elegant bones—like a treasure chest.

The glass-walled shower ran extraordinarily hot. I took my time with his clothes, watching planes of fair skin erupt from beneath black garments. I felt across his smooth chest. Traced the harsh, jagged ink on his stomach. Realized viscerally, carnally that I was no longer afraid of him. I'd made peace with my fear. There he was, my undoing, the master behind my derailment.

I've decided to be kept. The thought jostled around, loose and buoyant. *I am in the wasteland, unwilling to cross over.*

Steam billowed inside the spacious shower, cascading over him and I as we stepped onto wet tile. Darkness shielded whatever blood might've pinkened the water at our feet. I memorized his tenderness. The keystroke of his thumb on my bottom rib; how he fit the side of his palm in the cavern between my ass and thigh.

"Who did you feed to me?" I asked.

Jackson bumped his mouth against my cheekbone. "Someone unimportant. A software developer, I believe. Or the wife of one."

I wanted him to touch me, but I wasn't brave enough to tell him that. I wanted to take his hand and place it between my thighs, ask him to make me come while we stood together under the scalding water. But I didn't. I let him kiss me, and I remembered the way human flesh, cooked to perfection, had gone soft under my teeth. I let him wash me, and I remembered the desperation rampaging in my gut when I'd first woken in his apartment. I let him shampoo my hair, and I remembered how candlelight played on his fierce, handsome face.

"I'm going to keep you, Adrian," he whispered, holding me against his drenched body. The showerhead rained down on us. Steam, perfumed like jasmine and patchouli, fogged the air. I thought of God. I thought of Moses, and Abel, and Abraham. "I gave you an opportunity to stop me, or kill me, or get away from me, and you came back." I thought of Noah and kept my hands curled against his chest; my cheek pillowed on his collarbone. "I'll never let you go again. You understand?"

"I'm not something to be kept."

"You're not a pet," he said, sighing. "I know."

I stood on my tiptoes and pressed a kiss to his jaw. "You're here with me in hell, or purgatory—whatever this is—and you're never getting out, and you'll never get to make *this* choice again. You picked me, and one day, I'll open your chest." Each word rang in my molars. Vibrated my skeleton. Sounded wrong and *right*. "I'll remove your heart; I'll eat it raw. Do *you* understand?"

Jackson hummed. His grip tightened around my thigh, and he lifted, cupping my asscheek. "Listen to you, little dove. Making violence sound like a honeymoon."

I expected guilt to worm through me. Braced for shame and regret, for the immediacy of my choice to close around me like a beartrap. But when I thought of the light leaving Bradley's eyes, I felt nothing. I wasn't sure who I'd become. I wasn't sure of the skin I'd decided to occupy, or the self I'd emboldened. Several versions of my life unfurled inside me. God's plan. Lucifer's plan. *My plan*. I still didn't know which one I'd taken. Fate, destiny, defiance, coincidence. They were all synonyms now. Jackson turned the shower off and dried me with a towel.

"Will you let me do what I want with you?" he asked.

I walked backward, steered by his hands on my waist until my calves bumped the edge of his bed. "Depends. What is it you want?"

"To test the level of your resilience."

I peeled my tongue off the roof of my mouth. Warnings sparked and died in my mind. Excitement fluttered in my chest.

"Do you trust me, Adrian?"

"No," I said. Not the truth. Not exactly a lie. "But I'm willing to let you earn it."

Jackson set his hand on my chest and pushed. My back hit the comforter and I gazed up at him, poised like a meal or an altar. He studied me for a long time. His taut stature was completely still, only shifting for the steady rhythm of his breathing. How quickly my fear of him had dissolved into something greater, something honest. I tracked him as he crossed the room and disappeared into the closet. My pulse raced. I moved my gaze to the ceiling and swallowed to wet my throat, chasing the ache Jackson's cock left behind.

"On your hands and knees," he said.

I kept my eyes on the dark ceiling. *What're you doing here?* Inhaled a deep, grounding breath. *You will never be forgiven for this.* I rolled onto my stomach and got to all fours, digging my fingers into the blanket. *You are rotten, like Eve who came before you.* Jackson touched my tailbone. Smoothed his hand over my ass, between my cheeks, and rubbed my backhole. I kept myself upright and chewed my lip, waiting.

"Breathe," Jackson said.

I inhaled. He retracted his hand. Returned with slick fingers, pushing into me, stretching. I exhaled. I wasn't unfamiliar with anal, and I wasn't opposed to it. But I'd never been so thoughtfully prepped before. Jackson drove his fingers into me with care and purpose, scissoring his digits, working his hand deep. I stayed quiet. Breathed like he told me. Tried not to focus on the way my cunt ached, eager to be filled.

"You don't come until I tell you to," he said.

I cleared my throat. "Okay."

Jackson replaced his fingers with the smooth, cold tip of the metal plug I'd seen in his closet. I knew it by shape. By texture, too. He looped one arm around my waist, spreading his hand on the soft pout of my stomach, right between my hip bones. With the other, he pressed the plug inside me. It stung. Throbbed. I whimpered, gasping at the intrusive push. The plug's thick, lubed middle stretched me to a point I hadn't taken before. My hips jumped, but Jackson held me in place. Eased the metal toy deeper until it was properly seated. Relief bloomed inside me. The pain subsided, replaced by pleasing internal weight.

Before I could recover, Jackson reached lower, tugging on my swollen cock. "Tell me how it feels."

"Heavy," I mumbled. My eyelashes fluttered.

"And this?" His knees hit the bed and the mattress dipped. He slipped two fingers into my cunt, fucking me slowly.

A moan slipped out, accidental. "Good," I confessed. "Good, it feels—"

He curled his fingers. Rubbed my inner walls with hard, steady strokes.

"Jesus Christ," I whined. My elbows gave out and I buried my face in the comforter, enduring his swift, brutal ministrations.

"Like Christ, then? That's how it feels?" Jackson laughed in his throat.

My vision blurred. Everything dipped in and out of focus. I squeezed around the plug. Resisted the urge to trip into an early orgasm. I didn't answer. Just moaned, and whined, and spread my knees. I never wanted it to stop. This. Him. The way he touched me, graceless and rough, satisfied a primal hunger I'd never thought would—*could*—be fed. But maybe it wasn't his touch. Maybe it was *him*. Knowing what those hands were capable of. What they'd done.

A murderer's hands, giving me pleasure? A killer's touch, breaking me down?

Impossible. Miraculous.

"Ah, ah," he sang, and pulled away. "Not yet."

My body convulsed. I felt my cunt gape, slippery and open. "Please," I heaved in a shaky breath. "Please—"

"*Not yet.*"

I clamped my mouth shut.

Jackson kept me like that for minutes, but they felt like hours. He didn't touch me. Didn't speak. But then, like lightning, the *crack* of his flogger filled the room and my thighs suddenly burned. I cried out. I'd been spanked before. Smacked around by men who didn't know what they were doing. But Jackson whipped me with precision I'd only ever seen on video. The leather tassels stung my ass, bruised my thighs, left marks on my back. I trembled. Yelped, whimpered, gasped, and squeaked. Jackson gripped my nape and held me down, skipping the leather across my skin repeatedly. Pain left me unhinged. I was dazed. Unmoored by it.

Once my cries became shrill, Jackson dropped the flogger and brought his palm down on my ass, swatting me hard.

"What do you want, Adrian?"

I sucked in a labored breath. "Please," I murmured again, stupidly, childishly.

"Tell me."

"Make me…" I swallowed hot saliva. "Let me come, please. Make me come."

Something smooth and thick probed my pussy. It wasn't him. Wasn't flesh. The toy slid inside me easily, taking up space. I arched my back. Pushed against his hand, urging the dildo deeper. The toy was almost too big. Almost painful. But the lightweight silicone was just enough to make my eyes roll, and my stomach clench, and my groin pulse.

Jackson worked the toy too slowly, but after a long, drawn-out moment, I heard his soft laughter, confident and sexy, and cried out as the vibrator came to life. I couldn't focus. Couldn't do much more than wobble on my knees, chest pressed to the bed, knuckles whitened around the crumpled, green bedspread, and hold fast to Jackson's command: *not yet*.

"Jackson, please," I begged.

"Again."

"Please!"

"No, my name," he cooed, and thrust the toy faster. "Say it again."

"Jackson," I choked out. Heat built and broke inside me. I couldn't last much longer, couldn't hold off the pleasure coiled at the base of my spine, wound so tightly, about to break. "Jackson," I moaned, closing my eyes, breathing hard.

Jackson pulled the vibrator out and filled me with his cock. The toy still buzzed somewhere on the floor, but I could barely hear it over my own sounds, over the noisy smack of our skin, over Jackson's fast breath and harsh grunts. He fucked me without remorse. Used me like I was a doll, like I'd been bought at a price. I couldn't hold on. Couldn't wait for him to give me permission. My muscles seized. I squeezed around the plug, clenched around his cock, spasmed and shook. Pleasure burned through me. My cunt flooded, gushed. Jackson quickened his pace. He fucked me until I was sore. Until my orgasm was gone and everything ached. I went limp and let him have me. Stayed quiet and still while he buried himself in my oversensitive cunt and emptied inside me.

"I'll teach you obedience," he said, slyly, catching his breath.

I could barely move. Couldn't speak.

When he pulled out, I flinched. He didn't touch the plug, but he turned me over, flipping me onto my back.

"Don't scream," he whispered.

I opened my eyes. He was beautifully flushed. Unkempt in a way I hadn't seen before. Pupils blown, mouth relaxed, body sheened with sweat. He lowered a scalpel to my chest, just above the center of my ribcage on the left side, and pressed the blade into my skin. It was an animal thing. I wanted to scream, but I caught the sound in my throat and swallowed it. I wanted to kick, flail, squirm away from him, but I didn't. My back bowed, and my leaking cunt throbbed, and Jackson smothered my pitiful screech with his hand.

How he married pleasure and butchery sickened me. Thrilled me. Made me new.

The medical tool opened me easily. I didn't feel the cut at first. The aftermath, though, when blood seeped out, and my skin lifted away, that was when the pain came. It was scorching, dire, fiery pain. Explosive. Searing my torso. I stared at Jackson through blurry, watery eyes. Every part of me flexed. Every muscle tightened, everything inside me pulled toward the surface.

Jackson lowered his mouth to the place where he'd removed a piece of me and began to eat. The sliver of my skin softened under his teeth, and his tongue dug into the small, bloody cavern he'd carved out with the scalpel. I fought against lightheadedness. He loomed above me. Took my chin and jaw, and forced my attention, chewing slowly. My blood darkened his face.

Had I entered a dreamstate? Was I even alive?

Jackson swallowed. "You taste like heaven," he whispered, and kissed me.

I couldn't parse how I felt. My body was strung between fight and flight, satisfaction and disgust, hunger and delirium. I kissed him slowly. Blood, sticky and warm, caused our lips to glide and slip.

When it was over, it was over.

Breath deepened, softened. He set his thumb beneath the wound on my chest. Kissed my lips, and my cheek, and my throat.

"Are you mine, Adrian Price?"

I wanted to consume him like he'd consumed me. I closed my hand around his and took the scalpel. Turned toward him, straddling his waist, hovering over a killer, a captor, a thing mismade by God. I put the silver blade to his chest.

"I am," I said, because I'd chosen. Because I could never go back. "Are you mine, Jackson Monroe?"

I carved him. Split him. Saw him yawn open; red and beautiful.

Jackson stuttered through a gasp. "Yeah," he said, breath coming in puffs and pants. "I am."

I closed one hand around his throat. Squeezed.

Then I brought a piece of him to my mouth.

Chewed.

Swallowed.

And the dove came back to him in the evening, and behold, in her mouth was a freshly plucked olive leaf.

ravage

I took him on a Sunday. The Lord's Day.

Six months had come and gone, and Adrian Price was still the finest judgment I could've asked for, passed down from the mouth of Gabriel, or Uriel, or Michael, and delivered into my life from the kindling of Zeus and Mnemosyne. As cliché as it might've been, I was convinced Holy Father had bargained with the caretakers of Mount Olympus and sent me a muse. Someone who could strip away the senselessness infecting my life and bring me routine, surprise, *purpose*.

Adrian stepped into my ribcage like a ghost returned to its grave. Settled there, comfortable and imminent.

I thought of him as I stood in an old warehouse—easily rented for cash, easily ignored by police—and dragged my gloved finger over a naked torso. Heat still clung to her skin. The rope twined around her delicate ankles kept her body suspended, dangling like a slaughtered lamb. Her toes twitched, responding to signals sent from a flickering nervous system. The tripod behind me, topped with a camera and flanked by an oversized circle-light, captured every movement and illuminated the scene. Me, covered in industrial plastic, hidden by a black mask, standing before a dead woman who would soon be plated with broccolini and purple plums. I spread my hand over her stomach and remembered my palm clutching the back of Adrian's knee, how his thigh stretched toward his belly and his breath stuttered around misshapen prayer.

I clutched a scalpel. Pressed the silver tool to her navel and opened her slowly. Porcelain skin split for red, slick interior. I thought of Adrian's mouth. Visualized my cock sinking through the seam in her torso. Thought of Adrian's cunt and tried to imagine what her organs might feel like, slipping around me. Would it be like him? No, of course not. But I still pictured it. Remembered white teeth, glistening in the dark, and soft, midnight cries. Wanted to push myself inside a corpse and daydream about Adrian Price.

Sometimes, when he arched his back, or reached for a tall shelf, or popped his chewing gum, I imagined plunging my hand through his belly button, feeling around his crowded body, squeezing liver, kidney, intestine, lung. I knew how it felt, reaching into a person, excavating them like a diamond mine, but Adrian was full of precious things I'd never seen, and I thought about being inside him constantly.

I slid my hand into the corpse. If I didn't dress her quickly, she'd sour. Intestines fell by my feet. I removed her liver first, then searched for her stomach. I planned to slice the supple meat from her thighs and boil her bones for broth. I reached lower, working my knuckles along the backside of her ribcage. When I found the quiet muscle, round and oblong, I yanked it free.

Adrian had requested seared heart with raspberry sauce. He'd found the recipe on Pinterest and hadn't stopped talking about it for two weeks. *I'll make it for you,* I'd said. He'd looked at me through his lashes, doe-eyed and needy, and I'd known exactly what he wanted.

For six months, I lived through my routine. Watched, waited, hunted, collected. But I was no longer alone, and I saw Adrian's patience thinning.

I packaged the organs and meat in butcher paper and placed them in a cooler. The woman—a Pilates instructor from Los Angeles—swayed from the hook I'd tied her to. Her brown pony swept across the dirty floor. Blood pooled in the grooves of the plastic tarp beneath us. I stepped behind the leaking body, reached around to her front, and spread her flayed torso, giving the viewers on the other side of the camera access to her innards. I thought about Adrian's throat flexing, and almost gave in, almost shoved myself inside the lukewarm cadaver. But I didn't. I snapped a few of her bones and tugged them free, then cut her down and wrapped her in the tarp.

Somewhere off the highway, near the mountain range, I'd drag her into the forest and burn her.

Like all the others, I'd toss her ashes and charred remains into a grave and cover them in lye.

She would be devoured by the land, and me, and Adrian.

I got home late.

The living room was dark and different. Overtime, Adrian had tucked pieces of his life into mine. A monstera stood proudly by the glass slider and a few manga were stacked on the coffee table. His rose-colored blanket pooled on a couch cushion and his ankle boots had been kicked off near the shoe-rack. I sighed and bit the middle fingertip of my glove, tugging each off one by one, then set them in the sink with my mask. The fake skull stared back at me, hollow and alien. I let the accessories soak in citrus juice and soap. Placed the wrapped meat in the freezer; labeled the bone broth and slid it behind the oatmilk in the fridge. I sighed at the sight of Adrian's butterscotch coat draped over one of the kitchen chairs. I took the garment, smoothed it, and carried it down the dark hall and into our bedroom.

Our. The word stopped me. Caused my heart to pause, restart.

I stood at the foot of the bed and watched Adrian sleep. He was incredibly still—deceptively, so—but the slight part of his plump mouth, and the fine curve of his shoulder showcased his steady breathing. Soft, blonde waves fell over his brow. I wanted to pluck one of his eyelashes out and keep it in my wallet. I admired his face to the point of devotion. I fantasized about how his skin might fit over mine. I thought about killing him, often, always. But I loved having him too much to go through with it. He was my Tasmanian Tiger. My Renato Viola. I got to experience him. Watch him. Taste him, sometimes.

So, I committed to keeping him.

I hung his coat in the closet and stripped away my clothes. The shower ran hot, washing sweat and grime away. The blood flecked on my wrist disappeared with a dollop of soap. I set my palms against the tile and stretched my back until it popped. Rolled both ankles, cracked my neck, sighed as the tension in my body waned.

Last week, Adrian had asked Father Hudson to convince him the rapture hadn't happened. He asked for proof of *before*, concrete evidence of a life predating the book of Revelation. I listened to him cry and breathe in my headphones while I jogged through the park. I wanted to tattoo his madness onto my ribcage, soundwaves shaped like his sniffles and pleas. Our relationship had either driven him to mania or freed him from self-deprecation. He mentioned stigmata; he rambled about driving a nail through his palm. *Will it reveal Christ's vision?* His voice had trembled. *I already know God—a god—but would I find forgiveness if I emulated the suffering of our savior?* Father Hudson had told him to pray. Given him Catholic homework: Hail Mary, seven times, and an Act of Contrition, once, and fasting, something favored and habitual removed for long enough to be missed. After that session in the confessional, I'd made Adrian cry. Fucked him until he was red-faced and puffy-eyed, babbling and begging, overstimulated to the point of pissing and embarrassed over wetting the bed, and kept him shackled to the headboard while I read to him from the book of Daniel.

I loved him the same way hawks loved diving, talons outstretched, taking aim.

I dried myself with a towel and glanced at the mirror. I recognized my reflection more in the dark. My eyes, at least. But sometimes I couldn't attach myself to my physical form. Lean, yeah. Cared for; marked. Still, I couldn't imagine my body holding blood, despite seeing myself bleed. I couldn't fathom being full of mechanisms, all working toward a common goal. It was hard to fathom being alive.

But then, when I crawled into bed and Adrian cracked his eyes open, everything that moved, and bent, and beat inside me suddenly operated seamlessly. I hardly felt alive at all.

I felt held, though. Suspended in another person.

The only time I wanted to be aware of my body was when he was near it.

"Hey," he said, sliding his palm to my cheek. "What time is it?"

"Late."

His thumb found the scar on my mouth. "You okay?"

"Yeah, you?" I cupped his knuckles and brought his hand to my lips, leaving a kiss where he'd begged for stigmata.

"Yeah. Where've you been?"

That question was part of an immature routine. He only asked when he knew the answer.

I let the inquiry linger and appreciated his lovely throat and delicate nose. The early hours eased into morning. I didn't answer; he didn't ask again. He turned over and put his back to my torso. You'd think I'd be used to it by now, but it was still odd having someone warm and small pressed against me after spending years alone. Even stranger to hold him as I slept. I tried to imagine what he might dream about, and those thoughts became my own dreams—wine poured into Adrian's mouth, communion overflowing. Fitting my hand behind his teeth. Peeling away the tattoo on my knuckle and watching him swallow the moon. I dreamed about suffocating him. I dreamed about him decapitating me. I dreamed about our wedding, all the guests were faceless, applauding.

I rarely remembered my dreams when they were bold and fantastical. I usually dreamed about memories. The second time I killed someone, I went mad, I think. Lost all grasp on myself. I drank their blood and ripped through their skin, and when I dreamed about that transition, how the domesticity chipped away and I was *beast* underneath, I remembered the freedom of being unwell enough to become blissfully separate from reality. I dreamed about seeing Adrian for the first time, too. He'd ordered a chai latte and paid with a blue credit card. He'd worn a cableknit sweater and navy denim. I'd noticed his hands immediately, long and spidery. He'd enchanted me, and I'd known the universe would never let me see him again. I'd gone back the next day to call fate's bluff. But Adrian Price had been there, sipping a hot drink, typing on his laptop, and I knew a deity outside our earthly plane had orchestrated his placement in my life.

I am a jealous god.

I woke to Adrian reaching over me, hitting *snooze* on my alarm. Daylight beamed through the blinds. I touched his forearm as he laid atop me, sighing sleepily.

"I want to go with you," he said.

"Where?"

"Don't play dumb."

I hummed, tracing his spine. "Say it, then. Say what you want."

Adrian huffed. "I want to go hunting with you."

"*Say it.*"

Another huff, more annoyed. He shifted, holding himself above me. His wheat-colored hair fell into his eyes, and he slid his knees around my hips. He scraped his bottom lip with his teeth.

"I want to kill someone," he whispered, blushing apple-red.

I smiled. "Are you sure?"

"Yes."

"How?"

"How am I sure?"

"How do you want to do it? Tell me."

Adrian was loose and lulled, still waking. He lifted his hips and rocked forward, grinding his cotton underwear over my naked cock.

"Tell me," I repeated, lifting to meet another slow roll. Blood rushed downward. Heat flooded my core and spread outward. Him, like this, knowing he could convince me with pleasure, never failed to impress.

"You use a knife, don't you?" He reached between us and wrapped his hand around my hardening cock, stroking.

I grasped his hips. "Yes."

"I think I'd like that."

"Like what?"

Adrian pushed his underwear to the side and positioned my cock. His cunt opened around me, hot and wet, and I set my teeth as he sank down.

"Using a knife," he said. His jaw slackened. Pink cheeks brightened.

I spread my fingers over his waist and squeezed, digging into the soft expanse above his hipbones. "And what would you do with a knife, Adrian?"

He rested one hand on my chest and seized my throat with the other, gripping just so. "Cut someone here," he said, breathlessly, and tightened his hold. He rode me slowly at first, rising up, dropping down. I watched my body disappear into his with every rhythmic movement. "Look at me, Jackson."

I snapped my gaze to his. I wanted to thrust upward, bury my dick in his pussy, hold him still and make him whine. But more so, I wanted it to last.

"I want to slit someone's throat," he bit out, panting, quickening his pace. "I want to know what it's like to empty a body. I want to—" He gasped, grinding hard against my pelvis. "—I want you to fuck me with blood on your hands." *Oh.* I inhaled sharply. "I want to know sin in its rarest form. Give me..." He leaned over me. His cunt clenched, and his chest heaved, and my cock swelled inside him. "Give me the chance. Take me with you," he choked out, moaning, whimpering. "Take me with you. Let me do it, please, let me—"

I kissed him hard, silencing him. The thought of Adrian Price slitting a throat sent me spiraling. I wanted to witness it. I wanted to imagine it forever, on repeat. I wanted to burn the memory of it into my bones and revisit it nightly. I wanted the throat to be mine.

But I knew in my depths he wasn't ready.

Not for that; not yet.

I pushed away from the bed and sat upright, holding the small of his back. He wrapped around me, arms tight around my neck, legs open, hips jumping, meeting frantic thrusts. My control slipped. Sex devolved into the thing before lovemaking, the thing after spite. It was ferocious. Delirious. When I tipped him toward the bed, he shot his arm backward and braced there, making small, girlish noises as I drove myself into him.

I rested my forehead against his. Our breath mingled. Everything tightened and ruptured—his body; mine—until Adrian dug his fingernails into my nape and spasmed around me. His pussy flooded, gushed. I loved the way his swollen cock jutted from his slit, how I could keep him close and force his orgasm to deepen if I tilted my hips, if I kept him pressed against me, drenched and gaping. His cunt relaxed, slackened, leaked.

I pulled out. Adrian breathed like he'd been in a fight, but he didn't resist when I dropped him onto the comforter. Didn't flinch when I stumbled out of bed and pulled him by his elbows, dragging until his head dangled over the edge of the mattress. He opened his mouth.

"Good boy," I said, sighing, and slipped my cock down his throat.

At first, Adrian relaxed, tonguing at my shaft. But when I pushed deeper, he thrashed, clawed at the bedsheets, and tried to pull his face away.

I set my hand beneath his bellybutton and pushed until he whined, holding him down.

"No," I gritted out, working my hips in a fast, punishing rhythm.

The sound he made, coughing, retching, gagging, blurred my vision. Made me want to rewind the morning and start again. I watched his stomach concave. Stared down at his bulged throat, expanding, deflating, over and over. Saw him choke and spurt, sending saliva stringing onto his chin and down his cheeks. My body was alight. Every muscle tightened. The heat burning at the base of my spine released, and my head spun, and my legs almost gave out.

Perfect, I thought, *he's perfect*.

When I emptied into his mouth, he spat and sputtered. Everything inside me constricted. I gasped, grunted, thrusting shallowly, drawing out another noisy gag, another wet gurgle. I wanted him to swallow me. I wanted him to hold me inside him for hours. Once I finished, I pulled away, and Adrian gasped for air, coughing raggedly. His lips tickled my cock, trembling as he caught his breath.

"I almost puked," Adrian confessed.

"I knew you could take it," I said. "You good?"

"Give me a minute."

I stared at him. His messy lips, covered in come and saliva. Glassy eyes. Blotchy, flushed body. Sticky thighs, quaking. He placed his head on the bed again and gazed at me upside down. Tears streaked his temples.

"I don't need your permission," he whispered, voice raspy and unkempt.

I stepped back, leaned down, grabbed his jaw, and kissed his sloppy mouth. I licked into him. Tasted myself on his teeth and sucked at his tired tongue.

"Yes, you do," I said, because it was the truth. We both knew that. "You'll need a knife."

"Buy me one," he purred, dazedly.

"Fine."

"Good."

Adrian craned toward me. I kissed him again.

In the moments after, once we'd collected ourselves and wobbled to the bathroom, I detached the showerhead from the wall, crammed it between his legs, and held it there until his pretty knees buckled.

"Levine Law, how can I assist you?" I balanced the phone against my ear with my shoulder.

The patent leather chair squeaked as I rolled from left to right, and I tongued at my cheek while the woman on the other side of the standard office telephone blabbed about an unfair workplace.

"Ma'am, have you considered contacting your local union representative? Or organizing your team through a firm specializing in unionization? Yes... Yes, those do exist. Correct. If you provide a secure e-mail address, I'm happy to pass along some information. Yes. Yes, that's right." I typed her contact information into a blank, drafted e-mail. "Of course, thank you. Have a lovely day."

The firm was silent except for the click of my fingers on the keyboard and the sound of chatter from the shared hall in the rented business space. Everyone had gone home for the day. Times like that, when I was responding to emails, rinsing the coffee pot, and organizing case-data, I often wondered what kind of lawyer I would've made had I ever pursued a career in it. I had the mind for it, but not the drive. I had the backbone, but not the patience. The hunger, yes; the passion, no.

Me, dressed in a three-piece suit, prosecuting in front of a jury, would've been a divine comedy.

My phone buzzed on the desk.

> **Little Dove—** *what time will you be home?*

> *Soon. About to lock up.*

> **Little Dove—** *will you grab a bottle of prosecco on your way?*

> *Of course.*

I finished my last bit of work and tidied the front desk, securing paperwork and files in the locked cabinet. Even though I'd been busy with overdue cases and backlogged messages, I'd been ruminating on Adrian's desire to kill for six days. No number of record-requests or follow-up calls could quiet the constant stream of thought running behind my eyes. Adrian Price—*my Adrian*—carving a throat with a virgin blade. It would be a consummation. A departure. And I wasn't sure if I was ready to trade the man I'd taken for the man I always knew he would become.

I felt a strange kind of sickness about it.

I'd seen myself in him, hadn't I? Followed him, learned him, fallen for him. I wanted to savor that recognition. At the same time, I wanted to sharpen his severity into a sword. I wanted to wield him.

Adrian hadn't brought up our conversation a second time, but I replayed every moment of it while I locked the door behind me, crossed the parking lot, and got into my car. The 4Runner hummed to life. I let the engine warm and reached into the center console, retrieving a beautifully curved knife. The jet-black sheath clicked open and I laid the talon-shaped blade against my palm, turning it back and forth, watching my reflection skip across the silver surface.

It would fit perfectly in his small hand. Accentuate his grace. Make him deadly.

I gripped the handle hard and thought of him standing on the balcony, and stretched naked beneath me, and napping on the couch. A part of me wanted to keep him just like that. Mine, chosen. Another part of me, the worse part of me, wanted to shatter the first layer of his exoskeleton and watch him crawl forth, new and remade.

I drove to the liquor store with the knife perched on my thigh, then I tucked it safely into my pocket, found a bottle of Venetian prosecco, paid for it, and made my way home. I didn't exactly understand why Adrian kept his studio. He retreated there on occasion, disappearing for a couple days or a week, but most nights were the same: me, coming home to him. When he left, I'd go to him. I guess that might've been the allure. Me, finding him. Hunting him down again.

I tightened my grip on the steering wheel. My knuckles paled. Maybe I did understand it after all.

The parking garage was dark. I strode across the scuffed concrete and entered the apartment building, bypassing a neighbor with their purse-dog, and climbed the stairs to my floor. I opened the front door to find Adrian standing in the kitchen, chopping vegetables, wearing a simple crew-neck sweatshirt and fitted denim. He rubbed his left foot against his right calf. Mis-matched socks. Typical.

He switched his attention to me, eyes shielded by long, Bambi lashes. "Hi."

"How are you?" I put the bottle in the fridge to chill and came to stand behind him, slipping my palms along the gentle curve of his waist.

The way he moved, how he leaned into me, resting the back of his head on my collarbone, made me think of Eden, and flight, and simplicity. He was every good thing God had ever crafted. Like the death of a star, I was pulled toward him. All his light, all his essence, expanding until it swallowed me.

"Good," he said, snipping the stem from a carrot. "You?"

"Tired, but good. Did you thaw the heart?"

Adrian gestured to the sink. The organ rested there, still wrapped in butcher paper.

I trailed my hand beneath his sweatshirt, touching his soft tummy.

"Don't start," Adrian said, hushed and low, and pawed at my wrist. "I'm starving."

We'd entered a level of domesticity that I hadn't experienced in years. Sharing space together, cooking together, showering together, sleeping together. The routine baffled me.

If Adrian knew how quickly he'd unraveled me, how the transference of power had happened on a molecular level, on a biblical scale, he might've cut me down right there in the kitchen. If he knew I would put a gun in my mouth if he asked. If he knew I would slit my wrists, or leap from a building, or douse myself in gasoline, he might've lost all faith in me.

That was not how we were outfitted, but it was the naked truth.

If Adrian asked me to die, I would do it.

I washed my hands and helped him fix dinner. Oiled a skillet, sliced the heart into delicate strips, dumped cubed butter in with the meat, and added a stem of rosemary. Adrian reduced raspberries in a pot with chardonnay and honey and seasoned the sauce with Himalayan salt and a single bay leaf. We roasted root vegetables. Coconut rice simmered in the rice cooker with coconut milk and jasmine extract.

Like most nights, it was the tender touching that got me. The way Adrian tapped my tailbone and bumped his hip against my own. How he slipped in front of me to stir something and licked sauce from the side of his hand. How he hummed and nodded; how he was always accidentally smiling, lips ticked upward at the corners. The kitchen was small and confined, and our feet bumped, shoulders knocked, hands skipped across each other as we moved about, sharing the preparation of a meal. It was the kind of intimacy I hadn't prepared for. Simple. Undeserved.

I wanted to bottle the feeling. Sip from it when I was alone.

Once the food was plated, we sat down, and Adrian uncorked the prosecco, pouring fizzy wine into individual glasses. I looked at him for a long time. Watched him grasp his fork and knife and press silver teeth against the rare meat. Red sauce dotted his plate. His brought the heart to his mouth and chewed, swallowed.

"How is it?" I asked.

Adrian tilted his head and met my eyes, sliding another bite between his lips. "Earthier than I expected. Like venison, almost."

"Do you like it?"

"I do."

"Good."

I matched his pace and ate slowly, savoring the texture of the meat, how each bite came apart beneath my teeth, enjoying the sweet, vegetal carrots and the fluffy rice. I should've lit a candle.

"Do you ever think about hell?" Adrian finished his half of the heart and chased it with prosecco.

"Yes. Don't you?"

"Every day."

"What's your hell, Adrian? Fire and brimstone? An icy wasteland?"

"Drowning," he said, nodding. "Not in water, but... But submerged in something worse. Viscous, like blood but thicker. It seeps into my ears, and clumps in my eyelashes. It's slow. I think hell is supposed to be that way, though. Slow and repetitive. What's your hell, Jackson?"

"Starvation," I said, instantly. It wasn't the truth. My hell was absence. It was the place Adrian left behind when he ran off to his studio, the misshapen wound he punched through my chest when I woke without him. "I walk through the world unable to eat or drink. I'm empty, completely. Forcefully humbled with an eternal fast."

Blue eyes narrowed. "That's fitting."

"I have something for you."

His features sharpened and he sat straighter, studying me quizzically. "Is it a gift?"

"It is."

Adrian's cheeks darkened. He put his fork and knife down. "We talked about this, Jackson, I..."

I reached into my pocket and withdrew the knife. Adrian went quiet. He'd complained about my *bad* habit of showering him with gifts. Sarcastically called it love-bombing yet never made a point to discard the Versace sweater I'd bought for him, or remove the diamond studs from his earlobes, or throw away his Korean skincare. He still wore his Calvin Klein underwear, and asked me to order organic beepollen for his morning smoothies, and dropped twelve-dollar bathbombs in the tub without a second glance.

I loved him spoiled and well-kept even if he pretended not to.

I set the weapon down and slid it across the table toward him.

"You bought me a knife?" he asked, softly, as if he hadn't meant to.

"I did."

"I'm going with you, then."

"Next time."

"*Next time*," he parroted, breathlessly.

"Pick it up."

Adrian took the knife up with two fingers and grasped the handle. The way his hand wrapped around it, small and delicate, made the weapon look far more graceful than it had a moment ago. He tugged the sheath away, revealing the blade, and turned it back and forth. Silver caught the light like a trapped lake.

It was mesmerizing—Adrian, holding a knife. Like something I'd played out in a dream long before I'd ever met him.

I thought about the messy wishes and half-formed delusions scribbled in my journal. Maybe he was a sign from God after all. Maybe he was my departure. My descent into refinement. *Strange, how crucifixion is a synonym for pleasure*. The suddenness of the thought shook me. *Even stranger, how the reality of Adrian holding a knife renders me mute and foolish*. I wanted to place myself flat on the table. Lean my head back on his plate and give him my throat, just to see what he would do. Like a wolf showing its belly, I wanted to test the limitations of my lover's resilience. Pull him close, *so close*, and see if he would snap.

A part of me knew he wouldn't.

A part of me hoped he would.

I stayed still, though. I watched him flip the knife over in his hand and raise it eye-level, inspecting it like an archaeologist. I finished my sparkling wine and dabbed my lips with a napkin. Noticed how his steady gaze wavered as he put his thumb to the edge and drew a bead of blood.

"Careful," I said.

I imagined that knife flush against my ribcage and cleared my throat.

Adrian sucked the redness from his thumb. "Why this one?"

"Excuse me?"

"Why'd you choose this one for me?" He slid the knife back into its black sheath and set it on the table beside his almost empty plate.

I ate my last carrot and mulled over my answer. It reminded me of him. Small, beautiful, well-made. If I rested the blade on my palm, it stretched the length of my hand. A proper size. Its shape, how it curved like a talon, was birdish and horrific. He could open a body easily with little damage to the meat, or he could tear someone wide and gore them like a vulture.

"Versatility," I said, considering how I might reassemble my explanation to be a little more coherent. "It reminded me of struggle. Choice. Depending on who holds it, that knife can be artful or sinister, poised or barbaric. I've never pictured you as a butcher, so to speak, but I think you'll have range when it comes to personal technique. You'll be a shapeshifter, constantly stepping into new roles depending on who you've chosen to hunt." I noticed his expression twist curiously. "You disagree?"

"No, but it's still alarming."

"What is?"

"How well you know me," he said, so incredibly straightforward, so daringly *Adrian*.

I smiled. "Does any of this surprise you?"

"No." He refilled our glasses with the last of the prosecco. "You're the type of man who studies people. Even if I wanted to make you believe something else about me—trick you, so to speak—you'd look too closely for me to ever get away with it. You're inquisitive. You don't half-ass anything, even when it scares you."

"Nothing scares me."

Adrian laughed in his throat. "I scare you, Jackson."

I felt stripped clean, like a bone polished by a sandstorm. What a lovely, twisted thing to be entranced by someone, to be in love, and to be at peace with the fact that we made each other afraid. Is that how lions felt? How hyenas, and leopards, and sharks felt? In awe of their partner. Unsettled and destabilized by capability. Adrian had promised to kill me one day. I believed him. But I'd never taken the time to interrogate my *fear* of him, per se. I was afraid of so much. His ability to undo me. The way I'd brought him into my life as one thing and watched him become something else entirely. How often I daydreamed about flaying his stomach wide and sinking inside him. The chokehold he had on my body; the vice grip he had on my heart; the power he held in glances and whispers. I imagined he was the thing gods prayed to. The place before *beginning*. A precursor to inception.

So, yes. I guess Adrian did scare me. Terrified me, really.

Friday night arrived on the back of an early autumn chill. Fog rolled over Aurora, settling the city into the promise of October, and left Adrian and I seeking warmth in his studio. The gas-burning fake fireplace sent heat rippling into the small, square space. Adrian sighed as he struck a match and lit a cookie-scented candle on the coffee table.

I plated our takeout as neatly as I could, puddling creamy Dhansak curry next to a pile of jasmine rice. Adrian had wanted something spicy for dinner and I'd been too lazy to cook. So, we'd stopped by a local Indian joint next to the theater and ordered comfort food. Steam rose from chunks of orange-coated goat and diced vegetables, and the crisp *crack* of a canned IPA shattered the quiet.

"Alexa, turn on my rainy-day playlist," Adrian said.

The virtual assistant on the table—shaped like a small, round speaker—beeped. Music filled the studio. Soft, ambient instrumentals, acoustic guitar, and video game soundtracks. I smiled and sprinkled chopped green onions atop our food while he filled two glasses with bubbly, amber beer. We took our dinner to the couch and ate casually. I plopped on the floor with my back propped against the cushion and set my plate on the table. Adrian sat cross-legged, cozied in the corner of the couch with the plate in his lap. He looked frail and unbothered, dressed down in an oversized shirt. One of mine, maybe. Wearing sweatpants and pink socks.

"Do you think God will forgive you?" I asked.

Adrian lifted his brows, considering. "For what?"

"Coming back to me."

"Aren't you God?"

I heard the sarcasm in his voice. Registered the coy challenge in his blasphemous question. Laughter bubbled up and out of me, but I swallowed it down and shrugged, casting him a long look over my shoulder.

"What do you think?" I asked.

"I think you're a god in your own right. I think you're the kind of god that was worshiped a long time ago, and is still worshipped now, modernly."

"And what sort of god is that, Adrian?"

"The kind at the center of cult documentaries. Charles Manson is a god, I think. A bad one."

I focused on my food, gingerly scooping rice with curried meat. "Are you asking if I'd forgive you, then?"

"Would you?"

"Probably. Every god needs a saint. What about *your* god, though. The Father, Son, Holy Spirit. Would they forgive you?"

"According to the Old Testament, no. But if we're going by the New Testament, all I'd have to do is admit my sin and ask for forgiveness. *The old has passed away, behold, the new has come*." He sipped his beer and smiled, meeting my inquisitive gaze. "Corinthians," he explained.

"Would you apologize for it?"

"For what?"

I couldn't manage the truth, so I said, "Being with me," instead of *loving me*.

Adrian finished the last two bites on his plate and set the dish on the table. He shifted, placing one socked foot on the couch, and stretching his other leg across the cushions. He held his beer by the top of the glass, long fingers curled over it like an arachnid. He looked at me curiously, the same way a penguin might look at a scorpion or an anglerfish might look at a python. As if we'd never seen each other before. Like he was seeing me for the very first time or seeing through to a part of me I hadn't known existed. Something about it made me want to shrink. I wanted to fold inward and keep myself apart from him. At the same time, I wanted to peel back my skin and show him everything.

What have you done? I finished my dinner and got to my feet, carrying the dirty dishes to the kitchen. I rinsed the plates and listened to Adrian's themed playlist fill the room over the sound of the sink. When I walked around the couch again, I took Adrian's ankle and lifted his leg, sitting beside him with his calf stretched over my lap. I put my thumb to the sole of his foot. His shoulders loosened.

"No," Adrian said, and I wanted to believe him. The lie went rigid in his mouth, but I let him tell it, nonetheless.

I hummed appreciatively and worked my knuckles into his high arch. Cupped his heel and set two fingers to his ankle, following strong tendon upward.

"I would apologize for mistaking myself for someone who could resist you. If I'm God's design then he's expecting that, anyway."

"Expecting what?"

"Everything. Me, you, us. If I was given a choice—and I don't believe religion leaves room for that—then no matter what I chose, no matter where I went, God knew I would end up right here, doing this."

"With me," I said.

Adrian snorted a laugh and finished his beer. "With you."

As I massaged one foot, Adrian purred and unrolled his other leg, setting his ankle in my lap, too. We shared the quiet the way most lovers did. By firelight, after a warm meal. Adrian dozed while I traced his calves, and I finished my beer to the sound of evening traffic through the closed window. An hour passed. At one point, while Adrian slept, I stared at his chest, watching his breath come and go, and thought of faith. Where did it start and stop inside him? Was it an extra bone, tucked away near his heart, plated in gold? Was it a splinter wedged in a vital organ, pinching whenever he moved too quickly? I'd spent so much time researching God. Trying to understand the concept of religion. The lore behind an ancient thing repurposed for power.

And there was Adrian Price, the thing I'd captured, defining what worship meant to me.

He opened his eyes and flexed his feet, rolling each ankle.

"I have something for you," he said, hushed, groggy.

I tilted my head. "Do you?"

"Yeah. But if I give it to you, you have to give me something, too."

"Since when do you speak in riddles," I teased.

Adrian pushed away from where he'd sunk into the couch and crawled over me, setting his knees on either side of my hips. It was a strange thing, how I reached for him. My hands went to his jaw, thumbs tugged gently at his lips. I touched his teeth, and he slackened his jaw, probing my finger with his tongue.

"I'd make a relic out of you," I whispered. "I'd drill rubies here." I touched his canine. Held my breath when he sucked my digit. "Diamonds on your molars. Plate them in silver and gold. Archaeologists would want you for private collections. Curators would fight over you for museums." I didn't know where it came from, that confession, that fantasy. But Adrian smiled, so I smiled, too. "What do you want to give me?"

He leaned into my palm and set his small hands on my chest. Sometimes, during moments like those, when we were tangled in each other, dolphins in a net, drowning, I remembered how short our lives would likely be. One day, I would get caught, or Adrian would kill me, or *we* would get caught. Soon, we would be taken out by the police, or someone's father would cut our throats, or someone's sister would shoot us. Death was at our heels, nipping. I knew it; he did, too. But it was right then, enduring rapidfire *maybes*—marriage, and mortgages, and what Adrian's eyes might look like creased with age—that shocked me into subservience.

Could we be new? Could we stop?

Would we be what we are to each other if we became good people?

"A tattoo," Adrian said, and kissed the scar on my mouth.

"A tattoo? Like, from an artist or—"

"No, I bought ink and needles. Stick and poke, like good ol' dirtbags."

We laughed together, his mouth hovering above mine, my hands slipping to his waist. I wanted to lock our little life away and keep it safe. I wanted to watch him tear someone apart. I wanted to take a bath with him. I wanted to feed him, always. I wanted everything. I wanted to dictate a new law, a new place, a new eternity for us—*just us*.

"Where?" I asked.

Adrian touched my pectoral. Beneath his palm, a skinny scar striped my chest. The place he'd taken a bit of my body. Where he'd carved, and peeled, and swallowed.

"In Revelation, Jesus is said to place a mark on the chosen one's foreheads to spur the rapture. God brands Cain with an everlasting scar. Christ..." He took my hand and brought my palm to his lips, kissing the very center. "Wore stigmata to immortalize his sacrifice. I want to *own* you, Jackson Monroe. I want to put my mark on you; I want you to put your mark on me."

I couldn't stop my heart from lurching. Couldn't get a handle on the fiery passion Adrian had dislodged in my spirit. *Marry me*, I wanted to say, but I knew the cost of *us* was impermanence. Adrian and I were fleeting, like a collision of comets.

But I would love him while I could.

"Fine, but I get to make a request," I said.

Adrian sat back in my lap and waited, watching me carefully.

I licked my lips. "Mix your blood with the ink."

"*Fine*. You do the same."

"Fine."

"Okay."

My smile cracked into a grin. "All right."

Adrian blushed. "Good."

"Great," I said, chuckling.

He kissed me and slid off the couch, beckoning me with curled fingers. I followed him to the bed, only a few feet away, and lifted my arms when he tugged at my shirt. He told me to lie back, so I did. And when he lit two candles for the windowsill and one for the nightstand, I felt all the blood in my body rush backward. My head spun, dizzy with intimacy. Wracked with the impossible. I propped myself on my elbows, tracking Adrian as he flitted about the studio, grabbing disinfectant, a stick-and-poke grip, and an uncorked ink bottle. How could I extract the goodness from that night and freeze it? Store it somewhere ageless and go back to it again and again? Adrian met my eyes and every thought simultaneously emptied.

"Yours is darker than mine," Adrian said, tracing the scar on my chest with two fingers.

I nodded. "You were eager."

"Any design preference?" He arched an eyebrow. His lopsided smile twitched.

"Give me a sun," I said. He gave a gentle push. I eased back onto the rumpled bed. "To match my moon."

Adrian straddled me. He grabbed the knife I'd given him off the nightstand and cut the side of his wrist. It was a tiny wound. Insignificant, really. But it bled, dripping red into the onyx ink. He placed the ink bottle on the nightstand with the knife and lowered his wrist to my mouth. I framed the incision with my teeth. His wrist, so delicate, went limp as I tongued at the bloody slit. I wanted to flip him over and bury my face between his legs. His blood was coppery and slippery, like his come, like his cunt, and I wanted to taste him there, too. But he was intent on marking me, so I sucked until he pulled away, and savored the flavor while he collected the pen-shaped instrument and set the needle to my scar, driving the thin point into my flesh. I clenched my jaw. It pinched, stung, burned a little. But it was nothing like the searing, addictive pain that'd shot through me when he'd held a scalpel. This—him hovering over me, decorating me—was innocent in comparison.

He settled atop me, pelvis pressed to my own, draped across me like an artist. We spoke in hushed whispers. He asked me if I ever thought about leaving the country, and I told him, *yes, of course*. I asked him if he ever had nightmares, and he said, *yes, honey, a lot*. We told each other about our dreams, the good ones, the scary ones, but my mind stopped and started at *honey*, spoken so softly, where my name should've been. My heart thundered. I cupped his thighs over his sweatpants. Watched the candlelight play on his face, pinched tight with concentration. We talked about universes, and stars, and planets. He wanted an indoor herb garden, so I told him I'd get him a kit. I wanted to go to the opera in Denver because I'd never been before, and Adrian laughed, genuinely, and told me he'd go just to witness me there, in an opera house, dressed in finery. *Wolf in sheep's clothing*, he whispered and wiped my tattoo with a damp cloth. I could've listened to him talk for decades. About futures, and maybes, and us.

"Do you want to see it?" Adrian asked.

I shook my head. "Not yet. Are you ready for yours?"

He nodded. "There's another ink bottle in the kitchen."

I gripped his waist and lifted, moving him onto the bed beside me. It was excruciating—executing restraint. His mouth brushed my jaw and our noses bumped. Hands shifted across shoulders. I kissed his wrist, his temple, his neck, and he craned into me, captured my lips, opened his mouth and kissed me wetly, deeply. I ran my hand along his inner thigh. Let my palm go heavy over his crotch, gripping his pussy through his sweats. His breath hitched. I slid my hand upward, gathering his shirt, and worked the piece of clothing over his head, tossing it onto the floor. We enjoyed each other. Tested each other. Adrian kissed me patiently, daring me to stay there, to stroke his tongue with my own, to give into the heat smoldering between us. It was a constant thing, that fire. It stayed, and grew, and blazed. But I pulled away, intent on granting him the ownership he'd asked for.

His flushed cheeks. His swollen mouth. His half-lidded eyes. His pinkened chest.

I wanted to ruin him. I wanted to open him, and swallow him, and desecrate him.

This lovely thing I'd set free. This impossible man who'd come back to me.

"What?" Adrian asked.

I shook my head and got to my feet, staring down at him, sprawled on the bed like the subject of a renaissance painting. I found the ink in the kitchen and drew the black switchblade from my pocket, digging the tip into the heel of my palm. As my blood mingled with the ink, Adrian kept his gaze glued to the red dampening my hand. I kept him there, suspended, before I finally leaned over him and put my fingers between his lips, allowing blood to drip over my palm, down the underside of my digits and slide into his mouth. His throat flexed around a swallow. He stayed submissive, arms above his head, eyelashes fluttering, taking what I gave.

I smeared his lips shiny red. "Will you be good for me, little dove?"

He nodded enthusiastically.

"After we're done with this..." I held up the hand-poke tool. "You'll be a good boy and let me do whatever I want, however I want. Did you do what I asked you to do this morning?" I'd asked him to use the douching kit I'd left in the bathroom. He nodded again. "And did you wear what I asked you to wear?" He swallowed again, nodded again. "Show me."

Adrian pushed his sweats and underwear down and kicked them away. He turned over, displaying his ass and the black plug secure between his cheeks. His cunt glistened, already slick. He'd worn the training plug all day. To the coffee shop where he'd worked, to the thrift store, home, while we ate, while he napped. When I'd left the note for him, I knew he wouldn't disobey, but *seeing* it made my cock throb.

"Tell me what you want, Adrian."

"I want you to tattoo me."

"And then?"

His lips shook. "Do whatever you want."

"To *who?*"

"To me. I—I want you to do whatever you want to *me*."

How quickly we'd decided we were done talking. How quickly our interest in each other had sharpened to a red-hot point, driven toward fragile places. Sex was a language we both spoke, something tangible and communal we could use to break each other down. The vulnerability we'd shared throughout the evening stripped itself to the most animalistic act we had. Touch; being touched. Had; being had. Trust, somehow.

"What else do you want?" I asked, twirling the poke-tool.

"A feather," he said, "Or an olive branch. You choose."

I hummed and dipped the tool into the ink. The needle punctured his skin easily. He flinched once, but only once, and breathed deeply as I delivered ink and blood into his chest. I etched a feather into him. Worked mindfully. Kept the pace agonizingly slow, watching red bead up on the decorative wound. His scar was a beautiful thing, lean and pink, like the lines beneath his misshapen nipples. His body was an aging piece of art, cherished and restored, and I could've looked at him forever.

We didn't speak. Once I finished his tattoo, I wiped the excess ink away and traded the tattooing tools for the knife I'd left on his nightstand. I set the tip of the blade to his sternum and let it scrape him, skipping across his ribcage like keys on a piano. His gasp ruined me. The way his stomach concaved on every hitched breath, how he spread his legs and licked his lips, stoked my cruelty. I wanted him to cry. I wanted him to beg. I wanted him to never be the same again.

I coveted Adrian like a nun her vows, like a warrior his weapon.

There was so much I wanted, so much I would never have. But I would take what I could. Love how I could. Unleash what I could.

I slipped the knife between his legs. Slid the wide, flat side of the blade against his pussy.

"I'll need you on the floor for this," I said.

"Will it hurt?"

"At first, yeah."

Adrian stared at the ceiling, nodding slowly. "I've never—"

"I know. You'll be fine." I placed the knife on his pillow and crawled over him, working two fingers into his cunt. "Look at me." When he did, I fingered him slowly, massaging his inner walls. "I get to do whatever I want however I want. If you come, it's because I decide you will. If you cry, it's my doing. If you're in pain, I'm responsible."

He closed his eyes. His legs fell open and he lifted his hips, reaching for my hand. "How do you want me?"

I kissed him once, then removed my hand and got to my feet, pointing to the open space between the bed and the couch. "Hands and knees."

Adrian moved cautiously. He stared at the floor, glancing over his shoulder as I pulled on a pair of latex-free gloves. He shuddered at the click of the lube bottle and braced when I grasped the base of the plug.

"Breathe," I said.

He did as he was told.

I worked the toy out in increments, pulsing the wide middle in shallow thrusts. The plug came free. His hole gaped. He gasped, elbows wobbling for a moment before he righted himself. The candlelight hardly reached us, but even in the dark I could see his shoulders shake and his knees tremble at the intrusion of two, then three fingers. I wanted to reach into him. Wanted to feel him from the inside. But his body resisted, tensing as I slipped my pinky alongside my other fingers.

"Jackson," he choked out, whimpering. "It's too much, I can't—"

"You can," I snapped. "And you will."

Adrian made another pathetic noise. A mewl, a cry, something between the two, and heaved through a fearful breath.

I eased my hand deeper. "Easy," I purred, and placed my free hand between his legs, rubbing his swollen clit. His cunt spasmed, slick and sloppy. "Good boy. That's it... C'mon." Another push and my knuckles disappeared. Adrian grunted, moaning softly—pain or pleasure, likely both—and pressed back against my hand. I watched him swallow me. Saw my thumb glide inside and felt his hot body cling to my wrist. *There*. I flexed my fingers. Felt his body quiver and squeeze. "Good fucking boy."

Adrian sounded wounded. He panted, whining and chirping. His arms gave out. He flattened his cheek against the floor and sniffled, impaled on me, filled to the brim. He said my name again, "Jackson," like a plea, and widened his legs. "It's too much. S-stop, please, just... Stop."

I knew when stop meant *stop*. When no meant *no*. Sometimes the lines blurred between what he wanted and what I knew he needed, and sometimes the boundaries I set for him were swiped away like a line drawn in sand. That was what it meant for us to be lovers, I guess. For me to find him, for him to come back to me. We allowed each other the pleasure of defying each other's respectabilities. We allowed each other to *take* without restraint.

I withdrew my hand from between his thighs and held his waist steady, working my fist in a steady rhythm. Slow at first, then faster, harder, until Adrian's body rocked into each movement, and his moans became low and raw, and his eyes turned red and glassy. He was warm, and tight, and artificially wet, fluttering around my hand. I sank deeper, triggering his legs to violently shake and piss to stream onto the floor. He hiccupped on a sob. I anticipated as much. With his cunt gaping, and his breath labored, I knew his body would give into panic, would send signals it shouldn't.

"Stop," he cried out, whining, yet unwilling to thrash, to try and get away.

"You're mine," I said, setting a daunting pace. I listened to his moans grow weak. Watched him cry; watched his mouth part against the floor, leaving a puddle of saliva beneath his teeth. My heart thrummed wildly, and my head spun. I gripped the base of my flushed cock, relieving an ounce of pressure. "You wanted this, didn't you?"

Adrian didn't answer.

"Tell me you wanted it."

"I didn't," he said, sniffling. But he pushed into my hand. Sighed like a whore and smiled. "Please, Jackson, I—"

I slid my fist free. His torso bent toward the floor, but I grabbed his hips, shoving him away from the urine puddled between his knees. He clambered for the coffee table, holding himself up on quaking arms. I shoved him to the floor in front of the fireplace and pushed his legs apart, trapping him on his belly. I slid my cock inside him, filling the loose, slick space where my hand had been seconds ago. He muffled a groan against his bicep and lifted his pelvis, grinding against me. The tattoo on my chest stung. Heat enveloped me. I chased pleasure, snapping my hips, driving myself into him. I wanted him to feel thoroughly *used*. It was disrespectful how I threaded my fingers through the hair on the back of his head and held his face against the floor, and it was brutal, how I fucked him hard, fast, carnally, edging myself with his lax body.

Adrian went quiet, breath short and quick, and let out a strangled sound when I buried myself deep and spurted inside him. It knocked the wind out of me. I didn't come hard, necessarily. My orgasm unraveled quickly. The immediacy of it—coming, gasping, stopping—wracked us both. Adrian went limp. I pushed hard against his ass, enjoying the drowned feeling of his body going loose and pliant around my dick.

"Do you want to come?" I asked.

Adrian muttered, "Yes."

"*Yes?*"

"Yes, please," he croaked, so softly.

I wanted to stay there forever, holding him down, filling him. But I wanted him satisfied more. I pulled out and gripped his ass, looking down at his reddened hole. My come puddled inside him. I retrieved the plug and worked the toy past his rim, keeping him drenched and full, then I stripped off my gloves, flipped him onto his back, took him by his hips, and drew him into my lap. He was easy to maneuver—his legs gangly and useless; propped on his shoulders—and easier to hold. Light and small, Adrian fit against me like a prayer, and I tipped my face, opening my mouth over his cunt.

I ate him slowly. Licked his pussy with patient, firm strokes, and suckled lovingly at his swollen cock. Pushed my tongue inside him, swallowing salty fluid, allowing my mind to empty as he moaned. He held his hands in front of his mouth, relying on me to hold him up. I stared at him. His red, tear-stained cheeks. His fluttering lashes and sweat-sheened skin. *Gorgeous.* I flattened my tongue beneath his cock and sucked hard, listening to his moans turn shrill, watching his brow furrow and his chest heave. He shook when he came, dampening my chin. I licked until he went quiet again. Ate until he dropped his arms and closed his eyes.

I lowered his bottom half into my lap. His cunt left a wet streak on my stomach.

"Did I bleed?" he asked.

"No, you were fine. Sore?"

He nodded. "Can you get me into the shower?"

"In a minute."

"*Now* Jackson. I..." He gestured to the puddle a few feet away with a lazy wave. He met my gaze and narrowed his eyes. "You're disgusting, you know that? I almost pissed *on* you."

I shrugged. "A little piss never hurt anyone. Did you have fun?"

Adrian almost smiled. "I wouldn't call it fun."

"Of course, you had fun," I said, confidently, and scooped him into my arms.

He huffed as I carried him into the bathroom, and stared at me, dazed and sex-drunk, until I kissed him. I stayed with him while the water warmed, passing all the passion I had left into him by way of connection, lips and mouths. Adrian eased under the water. I left the bathroom door cracked and attended to the living room, leaving him to clean as he pleased. I wiped the floor with a dry towel, then a damp cloth soaked in all-purpose cleaner he kept under the kitchen sink, and dropped both in the laundry basket. I changed the sheets, too. Put the ink and poke-tool away, threw the used gloves in the garbage, set our beer glasses in the sink, then returned to the bathroom. When I came back, the black plug was clean and still wet, left to dry on the vanity, and Adrian was washing his hair.

I stepped into the shower behind him and rested my lips on his throat.

"You'll be sore for a minute," I said.

Adrian scoffed. "Yeah, obviously. Don't touch my ass for at least a week. I'm serious."

I bit back a laugh. "Fair enough."

He turned around. The irritated tattoo marred his chest. It wasn't pretty, but it was there. A small, curved feather settled over his scar. I touched the edge of it where his skin was raised and crimson, and he reached out to touch mine, pressing the side of his thumb to the rays stretching outward at the bottom of my black sun.

    Tomorrow, Adrian would make his first selection.

    I met his eyes, colored like a bluebird, and kissed him again.

    Tomorrow, I would teach him how to hunt.

"Where are we going?" Adrian asked, carefully studying the outfit I'd laid out on the bed.

We'd decided to get ready at my place and the sun had only set a few minutes ago. Pink and orange still saddled the horizon.

"To a party," I said. I gestured to the black masquerade mask on the comforter above his fine, gunmetal-colored shirt and fitted trousers. I had another mask for him, too. One he would wear after he'd selected our next conquest.

"A party where we're required to wear masks?" He arched an eyebrow.

"You've never been to a themed event before? They're full of livestock."

"Livestock," he echoed, laughing under his breath.

"Rich, groomed, well-fed Musk fans who lie about voting for Trump and publicly donate to green initiatives while investing in big oil under their private companies. Buttery skin, lean muscle, clean blood." I dragged my fingertips across his nape and walked into the closet, plucking my outfit from its place on the hanger-rod. "Would you rather find someone at a bar, babe? Liquored up and easy doesn't sound like your type."

"Used to be," he quipped.

"How're you feeling?"

Quiet came over the bedroom. I peeled off my sweater and replaced it with a crisp, white button-down and smoothed the front of a black dinner jacket. I peeked around the corner of the open doorway separating the closet from the rest of the room and fastened the clips on my dark, crimson pants. Adrian dressed slowly; gaze fixed on the shelves across from the bed. He worried his bottom lip with his teeth, and I wished it was mine.

"Adrian," I said, insistently.

He blinked, as if shaking away a stupor, and glanced at me. "What?"

"How're you feeling?"

"Fine."

"Adrian."

"You never get nervous about this?" He tucked in his shirt and pulled his belt tight. "Like, you never worry, or hesitate, or change your mind?"

"I've changed my mind before, yeah, but no, I usually don't worry. What're you worried about?"

"Prison, regret, police in riot gear, not being able to do it, freaking out, puking everywhere, being weak—"

Of course.

"Stop." I crossed the room and gripped the soft dents just below his shoulders, squeezing his biceps. "You've eaten what I've cooked, haven't you?" When he refused to look at me, I pinched his chin, forcing his gaze. He nodded. "And you watched me slaughter a man you'd been sleeping with, didn't you?" He wrinkled his nose. Nodded. "You know where I get our food, don't you?" He waited, stared hard into my eyes, then nodded again. I leaned closer, speaking against his slack mouth. "You ate me, didn't you?"

Adrian swallowed hard. "Yeah, I did."

"And I'll be there with you, right?"

"Yeah."

"So, there's nothing to worry about," I said, and kissed him.

Adrian softened and sighed. He tasted like toothpaste and tea.

I knew what the night had in store, and I couldn't wait to watch him move through a decadent world. He was such a fine, beautiful thing, so full of what I'd never been and would never be, twirling on the cusp of change. I tipped my head, stared at his jaw, and throat, and the shiny top button on his shirt. When I looked at him, I imagined Galilee. Desert palms, golden sand, clear skies. The birthplace of greatness destined for death. He reminded me of the virgin Mary, frightened of Gabriel despite his glorious message.

How easily a god could be forged, I thought. *How exciting it is to make one.*

Once we finished getting dressed, I knelt before Adrian and tied his shoelaces. I cupped the sole of each foot and slid his pointed, leather Oxford's into place, feeling across the soft cotton stretched over his heels and the strong cord of lean calves. The fond, quiet smile on his face was tender and small. He didn't rise from the edge of the bed until I took his hand, and we didn't leave the apartment until we'd both buttoned our coats.

The drive was easy but long, following a winding road toward the gentrified, wealthy side of Aurora. Tricked out Subaru's with roof racks and squeaky-clean dirt-tires hugged the sidewalk alongside fully loaded Jeep wranglers and top-of-the-line Land Cruisers. Electric trucks with trendy eco-friendly names and palm-sized Tesla sedans cruised by. Adrian tracked them through the window, headlights captured by the faint rain streaking the glass.

"How does this work?" Adrian asked.

"The party?"

He turned to look at me, clarifying his question with raised brows.

"I'll let you choose, and we'll go from there," I said.

"What happens after I choose?"

"We either lure, intimidate, or calculate. I don't anticipate it being difficult given the environment. Booze, music, sex, social climbing... it's the perfect hunting ground."

Adrian nodded. "And what will we do when... when we're finished? Where do we—"

"I'll show you everything, little dove." I reached across the center console and curled my hand around his thigh. "Don't overthink it, all right?"

His nervous energy soured the air, but I loved the citrus scent of it. How he rested his hand over my knuckles and held himself at the ready, watching people stroll through the city, unaware and unbothered. The eagerness stirring inside him was beginning to push toward the surface, and I was at once mournful and excited to see the horror he'd repressed finally creep outside his skin. I wanted to keep him just the way I'd found him, and I wanted to guide him into the next phase of his evolution.

He'll die if you don't, I reminded myself. *Great whites rot in captivity.*

I parked one block away from the antiquated mansion where the event was taking place. The alley was unlit and seedy, and we'd likely be one of only a few vehicles left there. I'd already checked the distance between the event and the butchery warehouse. It was the same place I usually went, rented in cash from a man well past his prime who never asked, and never said *thank you*, and never looked me in the eyes. The space was probably used to store illicit product, film illicit videos, produce illicit substances—I certainly wasn't the only one who paid under the table. I never assumed to know what went on in that dark, wide-open space, but I did like to fantasize about the possibilities.

"Do you have your knife?" I asked.

Adrian gave a curt nod. "Do we have everything else we'll need?"

"Sedatives, yeah. Powder and liquid. Put your mask on."

He did as I asked, placing the masquerade mask over his nose and eyes, and hiding the skinny, metal arms settled over the top of his ears with his blonde waves. It was more secure that way, positioned like glasses rather than tied with a ribbon. I followed his lead and secured my own mask. Red to his black.

"Is there anything else I should know before we go inside?" he asked.

I bought his hand to my mouth and kissed his knuckles. "Be vigilant and attentive. Remember, you're in control."

He nodded, eyes wide and unblinking. His throat worked around a slow swallow.

I locked the 4Runner, slipped the key into my back pocket, and laced my fingers with his as we took the sidewalk toward the old house.

The party was technically a gala with a focus on fundraising for sustainable coffee harvesting. I had zero interest in the coffee stain artwork or the faux farming initiatives that would make everyone feel just the slightest bit better about themselves. I wasn't going to bid on anything, or fawn over paintings, but I would watch Adrian move around his potential prey like a leopard released from captivity. And I would revel in it.

The doorman greeted us with a curt nod. "Mr. Monroe, thank you for joining us. May I take your coat?"

I handed him my coat before taking Adrian's and handing it over, too. Through the doorway, people moved about like living mannequins, stepping into flattering postures to garner attention. A leg outstretched; toe tipped toward the floor. Spine, arched. Chin, held upright, pointed subtly at the high ceiling. Cocktail attire and flashy masks; skyscraper heels and designer bags. A world brimming with a language I only half-spoke. Like a chameleon, I made myself interesting enough to look at, and with Adrian on my arm, eyes flicked our way once, twice, again, picking at our camouflage. Some of these people had seen me before because I'd allowed it. A kinesiologist from a dinner last season. The law professor I'd met at a work luncheon. A buyer from a high-end jeweler nodded at me, and I shook the hand of his colleague, a gem connoisseur with mines in South America and Central Africa.

Neither of them, I thought, and shot Adrian a firm glance. He nodded as if he'd read my mind and we walked into another room, filled with people admiring framed, top-lit artwork.

A classical pianist played rumbling, recognizable songs. Keen-eyed event staff in modest attire cut through the crowd, offering champagne, hors d'oeuvres, and mocktails. I rested my hand on the small of Adrian's back as we walked between each art piece, pretending to admire the brown streaks and faded splatters on canvases called *reinvent* and *early riser* and *upper*. I watched him study the crowd out of the corner of my eye. Saw his temperament sharpen, edging away from the anxiety he'd carried in the car and sinking into a fresh confidence I could only hope to continue nurturing. His patient, hungry gaze roamed, catching on expensive accessories and pitchy laughter.

"Jackson Monroe, hello," a cheerful voice came from behind us. I knew it well. "And who might this be?"

The thing about wealth—having it, pretending to have it—was that it came with being known. Doing what I did and being who I was didn't make perception an easy feat. I had to be seen; I had to be known. I had to keep secrets; I had to be an enigma. And now I had Adrian, who was tasked with discerning these patterns in the span of seconds. Who had to become part of a game I'd created, and played, and knew inside and out.

"Paxton Grimes, good to see you," I said, and rested my hand on the back of Adrian's neck, gripping his nape. "This is my partner, Adrian."

"Partner," Paxton said, surprised, and gave a narrow-eyed glance. "Didn't take you for a commitment guy, Jackson. Can't lie."

"Depends on the terms of the agreement," Adrian said, smooth as polished ice, and offered his hand. "Have you found anything to bid on yet, Mr. Grimes?"

Paxton briefly gripped Adrian's hand and snorted out a laugh. "Not quite yet. The crowd here isn't to my taste, you know. A little too uppity for me."

"Is that right? Well, it seems to be to our liking," he said, turning his gaze toward me. "But everyone has their own unique palate."

I tempered a smile. "Paxton is in the AI space, creating computerized bio-genetics with the ability to replicate cognitive human manipulation."

"Transgressive," Adrian said, feigning interest.

"It's blowin' up. Soon, there won't be a need for mediocrity at all."

"The student will most certainly become the teacher," Adrian said.

Paxton bristled. His sly smile cracked and he snapped his attention to me. *Control him*, he said with his eyes, *do something*. But I simply took Adrian's hand and nodded politely.

"Good seeing you," I said.

"Sure, you too," Paxton mumbled.

We walked toward a few large canvases leaning against the far wall, lit with exposed bulbs.

"Artificial Intelligence groupies," Adrian said under his breath and rolled his eyes. "How do you know him?"

"He has Levine Law on retainer," I said. "He's off the menu."

"*Cheeky,*" he said, sarcasm thick. "But whatever. Understood."

It was interesting. Ten minutes ago, Adrian was frightened and nervous, excited and out of his depth. But the longer he adjusted to the energy in the room, and the more he was exposed to the kind of people roaming, the more he sharpened, the more he stepped out of who he'd been and inched closer to the monster he was meant to become.

Adrian's evolution left me broken-hearted and completely enthralled.

Conversation lifted, sparking through laughter.

Adrian squeezed my hand.

"Oh, wow, like shit on paper, huh?" A slight, neatly dressed man dusted with white gold chains, fingers banded in glinting silver, came to a halt beside us. He was breathless, as if he'd been laughing, and shook his head, swiping his slender hand through copper curls. "Sorry," he added, flashing an apologetic grin our way. "But couldn't Chansey find a better artist? Not that I, you know..." He waved his hand toward the artwork. "Buy into any of this, but still."

"And who might you be?" I asked.

Adrian straightened in place, turning to look at the handsome stranger.

Well-built, I noted. Slender, but fed. Young. Clean skin, manicured nails, nice teeth. A suitable option. Easy, too.

"Oh, right, sorry. I'm Raye. William Duncan's my uncle, the guy who fronted this whole PR stunt." He waved his hand in the air again, signaling to the house and its occupants.

"Ah," I said, nodding. "Duncan Meat Refinery. Your uncle owns the controversial beef farms in South America, correct?"

"*Controversial,*" Raye repeated, laughing. "Sure, yeah, those ones. People want what they want and they want it cheap. He provides that. I don't really *get* the whole hoopla around poor public relations when it's the *public* keeping business steady." He gave Adrian a once over then turned and did the same to me. "Environments change. Worlds develop or they don't. And those *without* usually blame people *with* for having what they don't."

Adrian straightened in place, returning Raye's smooth look with one of his own.

Ah, I thought, and resisted smiling, *good choice, little dove*.

"I'm Adrian. This is my partner, Jackson. Have a drink with us," Adrian said. Flirtation was exactly the right path. He was a natural. I was impossibly proud. "Your candor is refreshing."

Raye cocked his head the same way a bird would. His smile twitched. Playful, hazel eyes jumped between us. "Is this your game, gentlemen? Find lonesome, rich suitors with foul mouths to woo at charity events?"

"That's exactly our game," I said. No use lying. I saw the glint in his eyes. Knew the chase was on. We had a different goal in mind, of course, but men with deep pockets and inflated egos were easy to seduce. He thought we were playthings, people who were rightfully beneath him, yet he was the one being hunted.

I knew his type. Young men like Raye found trouble often. They called the more established members on their family trees when it came time to bail money, lawyer fees, or credit card debt. They suckled at success like leeches. His father probably hated him; his mother was probably disappointed in him. They'd cry at his funeral after an extensive missing person search, and offer a hefty award for his safe return, and blame drugs, or partying, or the wrong crowd for his early death. They'd stop looking once the media coverage faded. They'd wash his name down with wine at dinner on the anniversary of his disappearance, and they'd hate themselves for being relieved.

Raye Duncan would have an elaborate celebration of life, but no one would miss him.

"There's a whiskey table around the corner," Raye said. "Coffee-themed, obviously."

"Obviously," Adrian parroted.

I nodded, smiling. "Of course."

When Raye turned on his heels, Adrian shot me a sharp, heated look. He was eager. I saw the places on him that wanted to split open—knuckles, wrists, the corners of his mouth—and tipped my chin, leveling him with a patient stare. *Stay calm*, I tried to tell him. *Take your time.*

The next steps required precision.

If Adrian panicked, we'd lose our chance.

If I missed my cue, we'd lose our chance.

If Raye refused our advances, we'd lose our chance.

During that finite, fleeting moment, success balanced on a paper-thin edge.

Around the corner, Raye grabbed short glasses half-filled with amber liquid from a crowded table, handing one to Adrian and then the next to me. Crystal glassware and fancy whiskey bottles spanned the back wall and complimentary appetizers—beef tartar, seared apples with goat cheese, burnt ends skewered alongside cranberries—filled the table. The artwork in the back room, likely a repurposed dining space, was abstract and pretty. Coffee stains shaped like planets, smudged like flowers, streaked like flames. I took one of the skewers and pulled a plump, red fruit, and some charred meat into my mouth, scraping my teeth along the wooden stick.

"So, what's your angle?" Raye asked. He propped his shoulder crudely against the wall beside a painting priced at ten thousand dollars. "Are you environmental reporters? App guys? Tech bros? Do you work for Peta?"

I barked out a laugh.

Adrian sipped his drink and licked his lips, arching a brow. He tapped his foot. His gaze, flighty and dark, moved restlessly around Raye. I knew what he was doing. Taking notes. Expensive, gaudy shoes with gold accents. Tight, tailored pants paired with an oversized button-down worn open, showcasing a long, gold chain. He was white, like fresh milk, speckled with reddish freckles. His meat would be a little tough, I thought. Dehydration from drug use. Brining would help, though.

"I'm in data analytics and Jackson works at a law firm. You?" Adrian asked.

Raye shrugged and winked. "C'mon, your boyfriend clocked my uncle. I don't work."

Adrian smirked. "Do you tell everyone you intend to sleep with that you're a trust fund baby?"

Bold. I kept my composure despite the surprising tonal shift. Hunger brewed inside Adrian. I sensed it. Could almost smell it. His pupils were saucers. Fingers drumming against the glass in his hand. He let his mouth curve upward—fake seduction. What Raye was being given was a show. Knowing what I knew, having what I had, made this part of the chase so incredibly sweet.

Adrian Price, beautiful, destructive, impatient, luring someone to their death—

Whiskey burned the roof of my mouth. I swallowed.

Watching him hunt made me consider prayer. *Thank you, Lord, for your gift is bountiful.*

I cleared my throat. "Excuse my partner's enthusiasm. I'm sure you're not—"

"No need to dance around it," Raye interjected, grinning. He tilted his head again, cocky and cute. His eyes flicked to Adrian. "Do you two partake in powder?"

I opened my mouth to speak, but Adrian was too quick.

"If it's good," he said.

Raye snickered. "First, I'm a trust fund baby, now I'm the guy at the party with weak shit? Make up your mind, angel face."

Fitting. Adrian eyed me carefully. Despite the overall hilarity of the situation, a twinge of jealousy still pierced my stomach.

Strange, how love made fools of us. Even at a time like that, blood pumping fast, adrenaline smacking like horse hooves, all I could think was *yes, my angel* and *heavenly* and *predator* and *mine*.

That exact moment reminded me of the Champawat Tiger. How she'd become a thing of nightmares due to a lucky bullet and broken fangs. How her revenge had been a natural chain of events following an avoidable action.

Raye did not know it, but I was the tiger in his dark night, and he was being led to slaughter by the very thing that'd chipped my tooth.

Once Raye darted his attention to me—*smart*, I noted, *paying mind to the decision maker*—I nodded.

"Sometimes," I said, and tossed back to rest of my drink. "On occasion."

"Sort of like threesomes, I'm guessing. Only when you're feelin' spicy?" Raye asked, shimmying his shoulders.

Adrian snorted a laugh.

I grinned. I wanted to tie Raye to a chair and give him to Adrian. *Do whatever you want,* I'd tell him, and record the whole thing. *Make him come, make him cry, make him bleed. Promise you'll let him go if he gets you off. Make him beg. Lie to him.* But I simply nodded, stroking Raye's childish pride. I formulated the step-by-step plan.

Getting him out of the party and down the street, into the car and to the warehouse.

"Exactly," I said. "But I'm sure you're used to being everyone's conquest."

At that, Raye's expression brightened. "You'd be surprised."

"Do *you* partake?" Adrian asked. Snagging Raye's chin with a bent finger, he turned the man to face him. "In threesomes, I mean."

"If it's good," he said. His blush was ripe, fanning across his nose and cheeks. He shied away from Adrian's hand and nodded toward a narrow hallway. "Bathroom's that way."

I grabbed two more untouched whiskey glasses from the catered table and met Adrian's eyes as we followed Raye. Adrian's fingertips brushed the back of my hand and an electric current hummed between us. This was it. Our moment. His time to become, to unbecome, to shed the skin he'd inhabited for a torturous half-life and fully free himself from the palatable, rule-keeping, *safe* existence most people desperately clung to.

The world needed people like us. We kept things in check. Made life more precious.

In the bathroom, Raye fished a gold-plated tube out of his front pocket followed by a small, round mirror, and set both items on the vanity. I locked the door behind us. While Raye went to work cutting lines, I set one of the drinks down and reached into my pocket, silently shifting the small cellophane baggie—holding a dose of GHB and ketamine—into my sleeve. It was a practiced movement. One I'd done many times. The drug was delivered soundlessly, stirred with my index finger, and kept close until the exact right—

Raye snorted a line. He straightened, laughing, and tipped his head toward the vanity, inviting us to do the same.

"A toast to your generosity." *There. Good.* I handed him the drink and took the untouched one off the counter, turning toward Adrian. *Now, distract.* I placed the glass against Adrian's plush mouth and tipped until the amber liquid soaked his lip. A bit dripped onto his chin as he swallowed. I slid my eyes to Raye. "And to our good fortune."

I watched his clever eyes follow the liquor from Adrian's lips to his jaw. But it was the long, steady pull from the drugged whiskey I'd handed him that triggered relief to unspool inside me, curling back like a loosed orange peel.

Adrian set the perfect trap. Became the perfect bait. Accomplished the perfect lure. I smiled, leaning in to lick the whiskey from Adrian's chin, while Raye stooped down to snort another line.

"It's done," I whispered, dusting my mouth along his throat. "Stay calm. Follow my lead."

Adrian's breath hitched.

As if on cue, Ray Duncan stumbled, catching himself on the countertop. He braced there with one hand and pawed at his eyes with the other, suddenly frantic, like most people were once their body recognized a lapse in control. He wobbled. Swayed.

Raye sputtered, "I'm... This—I don't know—"

"A little too much fun, I think," I said, and set my hand on his shoulder, steadying him.

Adrian, cool and stoic but humming like a livewire, kept his hungry eyes cemented on our successful bounty. "We'll take care of you," he said. I heard trumpets, and songbirds, and churchbells in his voice. "Don't worry."

THE EXTRACTION PROCESS WAS always the most challenging aspect of a hunt and Raye Duncan was no exception.

Once the spiked cocktail had taken effect, Adrian and I had to corral him through the party. While Raye's tongue was droopy and numb, and his limbs were heavy and unreliable, his eyes were still full of fear. Thankfully, privileged people—especially those with status and wealth—only liked to look at a trainwreck from behind a screen. When they were in proximity to a mess, they shied away, looked anywhere else, avoided the ugly until it was at a safely consumable distance. So, as me and Adrian guided Raye through the house, I watched the other partygoers turn away, shield their disgust, whisper to one another with faux concern. Even at the exit, the doorman frowned as he handed over Raye's coat, nodding when Adrian purred about *a little too much fun and maybe best to get going* and *you understand*.

Adrian expressed concern for being seen with him so publicly.

"That, my love, is our protection," I'd said, and drove us to the warehouse, paying mind to Raye's limp form in the backseat.

It was a dangerous, earnest thing, readying someone for their death. Like virginity, or ecstasy, or a rollercoaster, you never forgot your first kill, and the second, third, fourth would never live up to what you'd experienced with the first. It would be different for Adrian, of course. I had been alone; he wasn't. I'd had no instruction, no assistance, no teacher; he had me. We were together, ushering in a new phase of Adrian's life. Encouraging evolution. Trusting sanctioned desire.

And for Raye, we were delivering a terrifying truth: *you are not safe.*

Darkness flooded the warehouse.

"Like this," I said, and fastened a thick rope around Raye's limp wrists. "Okay, now, pull tight."

Adrian did as he was told, yanking until the knot fit in the grooves where Raye's wrists met. I hooked the rope around a metal hook protruding from the back wall, hoisting his body upright until his toes barely scraped the plastic tarp spread beneath him. Like many abandoned places and seedy, unlit storage stations, the warehouse was equipped with old holds, left-behind palettes, and broken machinery. The wall-hook? Probably used as a makeshift pully system. The ladder across the wide, empty space? Likely left behind after a stop-and-drop delivery of precious cargo. I tugged black gloves into place and flexed my hands, turning to watch Adrian circle Raye's dangling body.

"You're not a vulture," I said. He startled at the sound of my voice and whipped toward me. I pointed to the duffle a few feet away. "Get your mask before he comes to."

Adrian moved with a precise fluidity I'd never seen before. Like slow water, or the trickle of rain over a windowsill, body shifting into each mindful step, delicate digits drumming against his palm, lithe frame drawn to Raye in soft, natural pulses. He was everywhere all at once, making jilting, fluttery movements that left my chest in a strangled state—like standing on the edge of a tall building. His quirkiness, cast aside in favor of ruthlessness, hung from him like oddly fitting clothes, unwilling to be shrugged away.

I loved him for everything he'd kept hidden. For being wicked, and lovely, and deceptive.

"Where's your camera?" he asked.

"I brought the handheld. No need to livestream this one."

"Why not?"

"It's your first. It belongs to you, no one else."

"Then what's the camera for?"

I suppressed a smile. "After, maybe."

Time moved rapidly when it came to survival. While we readied the space for harvesting, Raye began to stir. His eyelashes fluttered, and his breathing came in ragged puffs through his nose. The effects of the sedatives ebbed, leaving a grogginess that only vibrant, thick adrenaline could penetrate. I pulled my mask into place, fitting the skeletal image over the bottom half of my face. Adrian placed a plain but theatrical white mask over his face, too, concealing everything from his nose to his hairline, leaving nothing except his mouth and eyes visible.

Raye gave a weak attempt at a thrash.

Adrian looked at me with a keen ferocity I'd seen very few times in my life. Once, when I'd locked eyes with another killer in another city in a quaint little bar where we'd both gone to find someone to hurt, and another time, during an argument with my ex, when she'd snapped her teeth and stomped her foot, as if the part of her that determined her humanity had suddenly flickered like a faulty bulb, lending strength to the *her* I'd always hoped she would become. The killer and I recognized each other instantly, like two orcas in a kiddy pool. I'd clung to that wild, unpredictable version of my ex until it fizzled out, and then I'd consumed her, searching for remnants of it in her marrow and rib meat.

Now, I looked at Adrian and thought *this is Genesis, this is godhood*.

"Do you have your knife?" I asked, keeping my voice even and slow.

Adrian untucked his shirt and unbuckled the slender sheath hidden in his waistband. He slid the knife free, turning the handle over in his palm.

"Good. Now, we want to spare the organs, right?"

He nodded.

"You could cut his throat or sever the femoral artery. What sounds more appealing?"

The atmosphere grew tighter, leaving me and Adrian in a space so small, so confined, that I could almost smell Raye's breath, could almost hear Adrian's heartbeat. Raye opened his eyes completely. They were glassy. Full of fright. His attention flashed to my face before settling on Adrian. He made a wounded noise, like they all did, and strained against the ropes, kicking helplessly at the plastic beneath his bare feet. Naked, I noticed how many freckles spanned his torso, and saw the way his body blotched *red*. He was flushed and dire. In a state of useless hope.

Adrian swallowed. He stood completely still, staring back at his chosen victim.

I wanted to read his thoughts. I wanted to possess him. I wanted to become the knife in his hand. I wanted to trade places with Raye Duncan. I wanted to watch Adrian become and animal. I wanted Adrian to sob and tell me, *no, I can't*. I wanted to witness greatness or to watch him recoil from it. I wanted to be his lungs—expanding; deflating—I wanted to be his blood. I wanted to fit myself inside his molars and feel him chew.

"Sweetheart," I purred, easing toward him. "It's cruel to make him wait."

Adrian's knuckles paled around the knife's handle.

I took a step toward him. Another. When I rounded his shoulders and walked behind Raye, I met Adrian's eyes in the gap between

Raye's arm stretched toward the ceiling and his head, hardly held upright. I snuck my arm around the man's quivering torso and gripped his jaw, forcing his chin upright, exposing the long line of his throat. Raye's Adam's apple bobbed.

I said nothing because there was nothing to say. Raye's muffled squeal hummed behind the duct tape I'd secured over his mouth. He gave a weak attempt at thrashing.

Adrian met my eyes, briefly, as if seeking permission, then flipped the knife over in his hand and drove it directly through the center of Raye's throat. It was unexpected. I anticipated a graceful, gliding movement, or a slow, careful puncture.

No.

Adrian—my sweet, holy, stolen Adrian—plunged the knife I'd gifted him through flesh, windpipe, bone. Blood speckled his mask. His chest heaved on a deep breath. He twisted the blade, tearing Raye's slender neck open. The sound bodies made always differed. Every death was unique. Raye gurgled and wretched and went silent. I felt the life leave him, coursing down and out. Adrian kept breathing, harder, faster, and brought the blade to his mouth, pressing the sticky surface to his tongue.

"Good job," I cooed. "Messy, but *good*."

The knife made a dull noise when it hit the plastic tarp. Before I could move, Adrian shot his hand forward, burying his fingers into the gaping wound he'd left in the very center of Raye's throat. He pulled with his thumbs. Yanked, ripped, tore, opening him wider. The mess grew, as did the ferocity in his eyes. It was a bright, feral thing—godhood. The taking; the control. Life was not precious, or promised, or fated. Living was as opportunistic as dying. It was luck and chance and nothing more.

One day, I would die. Looking at Adrian, I felt it more viscerally than I ever had before.

One day, Adrian Price would *slaughter* me.

I would love him now, and then, and all the time in between. Loving him, as deadly as it'd become, was compulsive.

Adrian retracted his hand. It shone slick and bright in the darkness, crimson, dripping.

"Moving quickly keeps the organs clean," I said, and dropped Raye's jaw. His head hung back, almost completely severed, and his gored neck yawned open.

I stepped around the dangling body and came to stand behind Adrian. I picked his knife up off the plastic tarp and placed it in his hand, cupping his wrist in a gentle, patient hold.

"I'll guide you," I whispered.

Adrian hadn't spoke, or moved, or blinked. But he shivered when I eased his weapon forward and prompted him to apply pressure to soft, freckled flesh. Raye's torso opened easily.

"Okay, now…" I took the knife into my free hand, then gripped his dominant hand with my own and brought him forward, pushing his fingers into the warm, slippery cavern. "First, what we don't need," I said, and pulled at intestine. Adrian felt across the sticky tubes as they fell by our feet. His breath steadied. I aligned my chest to his spine and rested my chin on his shoulder. "Liver," I whispered. Shifted. Coxed his hand to curl. "Stomach. Here…" Upward, behind the ribcage. "Lungs."

Bone scraped my wrist. Meat, and blood, and artery soaked my glove.

"You're gentle like this," he said, breathless.

It was a strange thing to say—gentle; our arms deep in death.

"Do you want the heart?" I asked.

Adrian nodded.

"Okay, so..." I guided his hand. "Here, near the lungs. Apply pressure—yeah, like that—and... pull..."

It took a moment, but Adrian loosed the muscle from its hiding place and yanked it free. He held it up, studying its curved, oblong shape. Slick, dark blood glossed his hand.

I wanted to know what he felt right then. He radiated strength, and vigor, and truth. But this was a new Adrian Price, bursting through the shell he'd been minutes ago, and I couldn't help the twinge of grief rippling through my stomach at the sight of him. I'd waited for this, for him.

So, this is what it is to create. I cradled his elbow, then his forearm, sliding my hand along his wrist until I found his knuckles, clasped around the heart like a jewel. *This is how Lucifer felt, knowing the fall came next.*

"How do you bare it?" Adrian asked. His voice was low and shaky.

"What do you mean?"

"How do you keep yourself at bay? How do you carry what you are around with you?"

I pressed my lips to his neck, tasting a fleck of blood. "Horns are just as heavy as wings, little dove. Angels and devils are one in the same."

"I don't know if that's true, Jackson." Adrian sighed, swiping his thumb along the curve of the too-still heart. "I don't know if God made us at all. We're different, you and I."

"I can't argue with that."

"Will it always feel like this? Like... like we're outside of it all. I don't know how or why, but I'm apart from everything now. It happened so..." He stopped to swallow, clearing his throat. "So quickly. I think I always knew, but giving into capability... It makes everything impermanent. Me. You. Us. We're—"

"Fleeting, yeah. The mark we leave isn't pretty, but it lasts. Even when we don't."

Adrian leaned into me. I took his weight, holding him while he sighed, keeping him steady as he unwound.

I said, "Lungs, next. Then we'll package the liver and kidneys. I'll take the thigh meat, too. I didn't bring a saw for this one, so we'll leave the ribs. Is that all right?"

He nodded curtly. "I want his blood, too."

"Sure." I dragged my lips across his jaw.

The quiet that came after a murder never ceased to amaze me.

I taught Adrian how to package organs. He held the empty Hydroflask while I cut the tender tissue inside Raye's thigh, gutting the artery there. The blood poured thick and sure. After, once we'd placed the organs in a cooler, we started the removal process. Everything heaped in the tarp. The body cut from the rope.

In the dark, surrounded by gore and horror, I kissed Adrian Price. His mouth slackened beneath my own, soft and wanting, and I found him changed, and brutal, and beautiful.

The lamp illuminated the living room, casting long shadows around my empty apartment.

I'd brought Adrian to the place where I'd buried numerous bodies. Showed him how the earth gave way in certain places, how to properly burn the dead, and how to cover a cadaver in lye from head to toe. I taught him how to dig a grave, how to tuck the corpse in close and pack the ground with turned soil. We'd stood together in the fog, searching for moonlight through murky cloud cover, and looked at each other as we stood atop skeletons. I kissed him with the smell of pine in the air. The blood crusted on his cheekbone looked like a misshapen birthmark.

Adrian stocked the freezer while I filled a plastic container in the sink with soap. I put my gloves in the sudsy mixture followed by our individual masks. The silence thickened, pressing us inward, toward each other.

"Will you run me a bath?" Adrian asked.

I didn't know what to anticipate, but it hadn't been the gnawing, unsure quiet stretched between us. It unnerved me, this hollow distance. Made me itchy for closeness. I imagined myself inside his skin, claustrophobic against bone and tendon.

I nodded. "Salt? Bubbles?"

He shook his head.

I took his chin in a firm grip and steered him toward me, forcing his gaze. "Adrian," I warned, lowly, cautiously. "What's going on?"

A sigh came and went, coasting across my chin. "Nothing, Jackson."

"Don't lie to me."

"Leave the lights off," he said, pressing into my hold. "Make sure the water's hot. Light a candle."

"Wine?"

He tapped the counter an inch from the Hydroflask. "Sort of."

I put my thumb to his bottom lip. "You did great tonight."

"I don't think it's greatness—"

"It is."

His lashes lowered, eyes half-lidded. "Do you think hell is all fire and brimstone? Or is it made of ice? Cold and desolate?"

"We're not there yet. We'll know one day, but today's not that day," I said.

"People like us don't stay alive," he whispered, bumping his nose against my cheek. "People like us—"

I kissed him, because he was right, because I didn't want to think of death—not ours; not yet—because I couldn't stand to hear the wobble in his voice.

"We're alive," I said, and pressed my lips to his again. "Now, here. You're alive. I'm alive."

Adrian exhaled sharply through his nose and cracked his eyes open.

"Be patient with me," he breathed out.

I said nothing, just nodded and walked to the bathroom.

It was a daunting, deliberate thing, loving Adrian Price. Loving him meant loving the hatred he held—the shame, the martyrdom. I leaned against the vanity while the faucet spewed hot water, thinking of his hand wedged inside Raye's torn throat, reminiscing on his narrowed, fierce eyes, and his taut, succinct body. I wanted to convince him. When I said *you're a saint, you're a god, you're holy* I wanted him to believe me. I wanted to dig into the wound his god had left and abandoned, and leave my own mark.

I have, haven't I?

Marked him, claimed him, kept him.

I turned off the water. Adrian appeared a second later and placed the Hydroflask on the vanity beside a container of hand soap. The dark held us. Shadow deepened in the corners and pooled beneath the claw-foot tub. I waited for him to reach for me. For his fingers to find my shirt, and his mouth to crane toward my own before I found purchase on his waist. We undressed each other slowly. It was his fingertips on my collarbone, palms flat against my chest, and my palms beneath his shirt, hands restless on his belt buckle. It was clothes by our feet. Skin and lips. His teeth snagged my cheek. He bit me there, like a little snake, and when he eased into the tub, I watched his fair flesh disappear underneath the water.

I wanted him to know power. I wanted him to feel worthy.

I unscrewed the Hydroflask and tipped the open spout over his face. Poured until the blood flowed over his brow, cheeks, chin, into his mouth, over the scars on his chest. The water pinkened. His jaw went slack and he tipped his head, baring his throat for the lifeforce we'd drained.

For years, I'd searched for something—some*one*. For months, I'd found everything I'd ever wanted in Adrian Price. But then, like that, he transcended the hope I'd had for him. Transformed it. I was terrified and transfixed. My pulse raced. I imagined I might wake up, but his eyes were too real for this to be a dream. His breath too warm to be recreated. Once the Hydroflask was empty, I placed it on the floor and reached into the water, between his legs, sinking two fingers inside him.

Adrian gripped the sides of the tub. His face—*red, red, red*—was serene. Eyes, closed. Lips, parted. He opened his legs, allowing me to sink deeper, to work my wrist in fast pulses. I fingered him until his breath shallowed. Curled and rubbed. Stretched him on my knuckles. When he moaned, I gripped his hair with my free hand and shoved him beneath the water. He didn't struggle, didn't writhe or fight. Just bucked his hips against my hand and clawed at me, sucking in a strangled breath when I let him surface.

Adrian sputtered. His eyes, unfocused and prettily dazed, lolled toward me. He hunched forward, held by my hand fisted in his hair, impaled on my fingers, panting.

"Drowning… You'd like that, wouldn't you?" I growled.

He tipped his knees toward his chest, granting me room.

I shoved my fingers deeper. Rubbed his inner walls until his eyes rolled back. That. *God, that*. The unrestrained pleasure on his face. That was what I wanted. Him, like this. Lawless. Desperate. Satisfied. I wanted him strung out and needy. Completely at my mercy. My cock throbbed. Everything inside me ached.

"Tell me you'd like that," I said.

"I'd like it," he whimpered.

"Say it."

"I'd like it if you killed me," he admitted.

I shoved his face beneath the water again. Fucked him hard and fast with my hand.

When I yanked him up for air, he coughed and floundered, holding himself up on the sides of the tub. "*Fuck.*"

I withdrew my hand and grabbed him by each elbow, hauling him to his feet. He looked confused at first but stumbled out of the tub and into the hall, dripping wet, still streaked with blood. I'd never wanted a person like I wanted him then. It was animal. Predatory. How quickly Adrian went from an unhinged man, tearing at someone's throat, holding an unbeating heart, to a possession, to a pet. It was impossible. It drove me mad. His submission, his acquiescence, his eagerness to be pleased, to be used.

Perfect, I thought. *Ruined and perfect.*

Because of the blood, I would have to burn whatever bedding we touched, so I guided him into the guest room and threw him down on the bed. He landed on his stomach. I didn't give him time to move. Couldn't spare a single moment. I crawled onto the bed behind him, seized his hips, and drove my cock into his cunt.

Adrian gasped. The noise that left his throat shattered the quiet, raspy and unrestrained. I splayed my hand over the side of his skull, fingers threaded through his hair, and held him down. His chest was flat against the bed, knees bent, legs wide. My thumb curved across his face and plucked at the corner of his mouth. Like that, looking down at glassy, lulled eyes, bloodied face, blushing skin, I thought of idolatry and false gods, worship and betrayal.

How jealous God must be, watching me give all my faith to Adrian Price.

I snapped my hips. Drove myself into his body again and again, faster, without control. Until the sound of our skin meeting was as loud as his cries. Until the way his body convulsed and squeezed was all I could feel. Until he was moaning and mewling, easy to use, warm and drenched, knuckles white, clutching the blanket.

"Jackson, please." His voice was pitchy and raw.

I paused, turning him onto his back and wrapped my hand around his throat. He reached for me with his hips, pushing his slick, empty pussy toward me.

I crawled over him, though. Positioned my cock in front of his mouth and moved my hand from his throat to the back of his head, holding him still. He struggled to look up at me. Struggled to swallow around me. Struggled to stay still while I pumped between his lips, fucking his spit-slicked mouth. But once we were there, rhythmic and entranced, he gave up any control he had left. He was beautiful like that—gagging, slurping—and even more beautiful when I pulled out. He opened his mouth, heaving, accepting the warm spurt of my spunk on his tongue, across his nose, splattered on his cheeks. Pleasure threw me into tremors. I braced on the headboard with one hand and kept him still with the other, allowing him to work my cock in firm, fast strokes. It was explosive. Lasting. The kind of orgasm that caused my head to spin.

"Show me," I said, catching my breath. I let him go.

Adrian rested his head on the bed and opened his mouth wider, displaying the come puddled on his tongue, stringing between his top and bottom teeth.

"You're a fucking blessing," I whispered. I sat back on my heels and eased my hand between his legs again, sinking three fingers inside him. I kept my fingers deep, massaging his cunt. "Look at me, Adrian." He did as he was told. My come, caked on his face. His mouth, open and reddened. Tears streaked his cheeks. "You'll never need to seek forgiveness from me, understood? I'm a giving god." I bent my fingers. Palmed his sweet cunt and rubbed his cock. "I'm the only god you need. Say it."

Adrian whimpered. He tried to close his legs, but I shoved them apart and caged him against the bed, hovering above him.

"Say it."

"You're my god," he gasped out, shaking and whining.

"Again."

"You're my god, Jackson. *You're my god*, you're—"

I fucked him through a messy orgasm. His eyes rolled and he sucked in a sharp breath, crying out as his cunt squeezed and flooded. He sprayed, gushing over my hand. His stomach lurched and he bowed off the bed, noise dimming, trapped in a breathless shout. I loved the sound of his pussy, slippery and overworked, and the way he clawed at the bed, and how he finally said my name again. *Jackson*, like wreckage. Like he was in turmoil.

When I stopped, he finally took a breath.

I brought my hand from his cunt to his face and gripped his jaw, kissing him hard on the mouth.

"Do you love me?" he asked, so weakly.

I am obsessed with you. I want to be you. Kill me, Adrian. Find immortality with me. I will never let you go. Stay, stay, stay.

"Yeah, Adrian. I love you dearly."

Adrian went limp, sinking pleasantly into the bed. I tasted him, and myself, and someone else. Us; blood. Sacrifice. Religion.

"Do you love me?" I asked. Fear speared me.

Adrian huffed out a laugh, as if I'd asked the impossible. He smoothed his hand across my face. Covered my eyes with his palm, then dropped it to my chest and cupped my tattoo.

"I love you, Jackson," he whispered. "How could I not?"

The question was rhetorical. So many easy answers.

I kissed him again. Tasted future, inevitability, fate.

"Cook me something," he said against my lips. "I'm starving."

Do not be conformed to this world, but be transformed by the renewal of your mind, that by testing you may discern what is the will of God, what is good and acceptable and perfect.

ADRIAN PRICE

On a Tuesday afternoon, Jackson Monroe studied me, leaning his hip against the kitchen counter, arms crossed, mouth set in a stern, straight line. He'd been marinating six freshly thawed ribs in lime juice, vinegar, and cherry soda when he'd asked me what was wrong. I hadn't answered because I hadn't wanted to. Because telling him would likely spur a game of introspection—he would pry me open like an oyster; I would become soft and cold, manipulated into compliance by the man I loved.

But now, we were at an impasse. I sat on the sofa, pretending to read a dog-eared volume of Chainsaw Man, bathed in the blanched light of a newborn summer. And Jackson watched like a wolf, hardly breathing, waiting for me to indulge his morbid curiosity. He didn't like being ignored. It was something I'd learned about him like a mouse learns how to nibble bait around a snap-trap. Still, I kept my eyes pinned to the black-and-white page and stayed silent, waiting for him to turn back to our dinner preparations.

"Adrian," he said, concerned, framing my name the same way someone would say *now* or *stop*.

I lifted my gaze and glanced at him.

Jackson did as I thought. He placed a teal lid on the glass Tupperware, closed it, and slid the packaged meat into the fridge to continue soaking. I hadn't considered his invasiveness, even though I should've.

Hadn't thought about how quickly he would wash his hands, dry them with a dishcloth, and walk into the living room. When he stepped in front of me and snatched my jaw, his hold was firm but gentle, and when he grasped my book with his free hand and snapped it shut, I did nothing but roll my eyes.

Of course, there was no getting away with it. No keeping it to myself. No burying it deep, festering in it, and letting it sour me for the rest of the day. Not anymore. Not with Jackson Monroe at my side.

I should've known better, truly.

"Adrian," he said again, softer, like a command. He kept my chin cradled in his palm and held me there, face tilted upward, attention surrendered by force.

How cathartic to be handled so lovingly, so possessively.

"It's my mother's birthday," I said.

Together for nine months, me and him, as long as it'd taken for me to gestate in her belly. I'd been a perfect little girl who'd stepped out of her womanhood and become a man by choice, curdling every ounce of whatever love my mother had put on reserve for me. She was cold and vicious, but she had been the first thing I'd cried out for as a newborn, the first thing I'd called to, the first thing I'd clung to, the first thing I'd lost. A part of me loved her, somehow. Missed her, even. I imagined her birthday cake—pink, modest—served with canned peaches and vanilla ice cream. I thought of the gold crucifix she wore around her neck, identical to mine. We would've prayed before cutting the cake. She would've thanked the Almighty Lord for her beautiful family, and her healthy daughter, and her precious life, and we would've said *amen*, smiling, believing it.

Jackson smoothed his thumb across my mouth, silently asking for more. Like a small, silver spoon jammed under my shell, lifting, searching for a pearl.

"She named me Andrea," I blurted, granting him a weapon.

I meant to say *today is the only day I ever miss her*, but I said my deadname instead, letting those three strange, unfamiliar syllables fall between us. Something sweet, spilled. I blinked. My brow cinched with confusion, but I hadn't the slightest clue why. Couldn't understand the reason I'd said it, why it'd needed to be said. But Jackson looked pleased with the information, if not a bit confused himself. He tugged at my bottom lip and sighed, tilting his head.

"Doesn't suit you," he said.

"Never did."

"Adrian—"

"She hated me—*hates* me." I swallowed painfully, dislodging the stone in my throat. "We haven't spoken in years, but I know she does. Bet she stopped prayin' for me."

"You don't need her prayers."

"She's my mom," I said, yelpish and wounded.

Jackson inhaled a great, deep breath through his nose, and the edges of his lips twitched upright.

Oh, you're hurt, his expression said, as if he'd picked a lock as if he'd intruded. But this was a part of me he'd yet to see. He'd held me through the night, and suckled wetly at my cunt, and licked blood from his fingertips. He'd felt around inside me like a cadaver, looking for new things to grab, squeeze, and claim, but he'd never found the well-hidden sliver of my mother.

She'd been born on the fourth of June, sometime before the economy crashed, sometime after the towers fell. So, every morning, when I woke on June fourth, I remembered that I once had a mother who cherished me, who would've choked the world for me, who would've died for me, who in an instant—after one, single, monumental conversation—decided I was no longer hers. I had reclaimed myself, she'd told me. People like me had no right to a mother, because they were birthless, remade in the image of the betrayer, the defiler. Denying what God had granted me was a sin she could not forgive. My father, a wise, lucid man, knew better than to choose a child who could leave him over the woman who was contractually and spiritually obligated to him.

If he'd taken my side, if he'd turned on her, who would wash his clothes? And feed him? And be his whetstone?

Perhaps my father had seen it in my eyes, my unwillingness to ever step into my mother's shoes, or maybe he'd seen me as exclusively a part of her, like a tumor, like a teratoma. Truthfully, I had always felt closer to my mother, anyway. Sometimes I dug in my bellybutton, searching for the cord that used to tie me to her.

I looked at Jackson—who had seen monstrosity stirring beneath my skin and unleashed it—and tried to make peace with his innate ability to find my weaknesses. Even after all this time, it was comforting and surprising how he exploited my innermost demons and gave them teeth.

Gently, Jackson asked, "Is that all?"

I wanted to bite his hand, but I stayed perfectly still, waiting for him to finish inspecting my pain. Sometimes his love was clinical. Sometimes it felt like peroxide.

"You could have a little compassion, Jackson," I said, finally, after an eternity.

He tipped his head. Like a bird, his eyes sharpened.

Yes, I'm hurt, I wanted to say. *Yes, it's trivial, nonsensical pain. Yes, I understand it doesn't serve me. Yes, yes, you're right, I know. Let me have it. It's mine, it's mine, it's all I have left of her.* But I didn't—of course, I didn't.

I didn't know what to expect in that moment. That he might return to the kitchen and ignore my existence for the rest of the night. That he might run himself a bath and leave me to my grief. That he might calmly and sternly tell me to explain myself to him, all the ruin, all the upheaval, until I cried.

Carefully, he moved his hand and cupped my cheek, steadying me before he leaned down and kissed my slack mouth.

It was a tender, trying kiss. An apology, maybe. Or something close enough to garner forgiveness.

"Do you want to talk about it?" Jackson asked.

I shook my head. "I want to get away from it."

"C'mon, little dove, that's all you had to say."

I let him pull me off the sofa and allowed myself to be maneuvered however he pleased. His wide hands drifted underneath my shirt, framing my spine. His thumbs worked at bone and muscle. Like a stray used to being fed, I returned to him, obedient and hopeful, and he held onto me, quiet and attentive. I'd expected his excavation of my past to be studious. Thoughtful, even. I'd braced for an argument. For clipped words and dissection. But Jackson put his lips to my cheekbone, then lower, against my pulse, and gathered my tired, flighty body against his own.

When I coiled my arms around his neck, he brought me closer, squeezing, and when I pushed my fingers through the buzzed hair at the base of his neck, he purred. It was alien—deceptive, almost—how brazenly I desired him. How wanting him was an eclipse, shadowing every thought, every whim, every shred of pain I'd clutched seconds, minutes, hours ago. I'd woken thinking *I am an orphan*. But right then, I thought of nothing except Jackson Monroe, how he could've cracked me like a wishbone, how he could've worn me down, crushed my pain beneath his heel and demanded an explanation for it.

But instead, he treated me delicately, like porcelain, like a thing with hollow bones.

We stood in the living room for a long time, holding onto each other, silently feeling across shoulders and spine, bicep and ribcage. I should've known he was built for this, too. I should've put my faith in his ability to become exactly what I needed without hesitation.

Jackson was not always gentle, or sensitive, or soft, but he never failed to show me care, and when I was at a point where gentleness, and sensitivity, and softness were requirements, he gave them to me with the utmost ease.

Love was a devilish, brilliant thing with him. Sometimes I woke thinking of the things we'd done, the things we would do, and wept in a confessional, denouncing the damnation I knew we'd earned. Sometimes I felt more alive than I'd ever been, simply riding in the passenger's seat with his hand on my thigh. Sometimes I thought about marrying him; sometimes I thought about murdering him.

Right then, the thought of being without him ran through me like a spear, and I found myself groping him like a lifeline, like an addict, like a little child.

It was my mother's birthday, after all, and I was reminded that the first person who'd looked at me, who had been biologically designed to love me, had stopped caring for me with a startling quickness. But this man, this beast, this nightmare of a person had hunted me down, and collected me, and kept me, and decided to love me loudly, and passionately, and without pause.

I gripped his nape and searched for his mouth. He met me tenderly. I wondered about romance and justice, and where the two intersected. How I couldn't decipher the consequence that came with loving him; how I didn't know what the universe had in store for such wretchedness.

So, I would squeeze all the juice out with clumsy hands. I would consume what we'd relinquished to each other with cruel insatiability. *I would have him*, I thought, *I would be had*.

"Come here," he murmured, sincerity so sweet it sparked like a livewire in my chest.

Jackson picked me up, hands snug beneath my ass, and carried me into the hall.

With my back against the wall, my thighs around his hips, my hands in his hair, I knew freedom. With his breath hot on my teeth, fingers digging into supple skin, tongue sure and searching, I remembered that I was an obsession. The object of his affection, the unraveling of his self-control, the determination of his madness.

I was Adrian Price who had survived Jackson Monroe.

He kissed me slowly, like he rarely did. He widened his jaw and licked into my mouth, forcing heat and lust down my throat. His lips slipped across mine; his pelvis pressed against my crotch; everything slowed, and stretched, and succumbed.

"Let me take care of you," he said, kissing me again, grinding the hard line trapped inside his jeans between my legs.

I nodded. I didn't want to think. I didn't want to trap myself in the annual cycle of grief, and heartbreak, and animosity that June fourth usually brought. Not when I had Jackson.

Usually, we fucked ritualistically, like animals after feeding, like acolytes after service. Sometimes we played, laughing, and tumbling about, holding each other down and experimenting with toys and restraints. Sometimes we punished, bit, and clawed, ruthless with each other, leaving soreness and bruises behind. Sometimes Jackson brought me to tears, or guided me to the edge of delusion, pleasure-drunk and foolish. Sometimes he scared me, too. Drove a blade too deep. Ate too eagerly from my flesh, tearing at wounds with his canines, wolfish, crazed.

But that Tuesday afternoon, he lowered me onto the bed while our lips were still connected. Undressed me with the utmost patience, tugging at my pants, pressing his mouth to the side of my foot as he peeled away one sock, then the other. Nuzzled my calf, and scraped his teeth across my hip bone, and took my nipple into his mouth. The sensation in my chest had dwindled after top surgery—something I terribly missed—but I arched into him anyway, relishing the twinge of pleasure that hummed beneath my taut skin. He opened his mouth over the healed tattoo he'd etched atop the first scar he'd given me, and brought his naked body over mine, pressing me into the forest-green comforter.

Making love was not an act we engaged in often. Never intentional; always accidental. A midnight coupling, or a bit of slow, morning pleasure. But that afternoon, Jackson made love to me on purpose. He touched me reverently, easing his hand between my legs, sinking two fingers into my cunt. Kept his digits deep, massaging my inner walls. Made me gasp and keen, and kept me close, getting me wet and eager before replacing his fingers with his cock.

He rested his forehead against mine, breath coasting my open mouth, gaze locked with my own, and met every movement with intent. I rolled my hips, and he ground against my cock, establishing a toe-curling rhythm.

"My pretty boy," he whispered, lips gentle on my temple, then my ear. "Tell me something true."

"I love you," I said, breathless, and framed his neck between my hands, holding onto him.

Jackson nibbled my earlobe. "Would you marry me, Adrian?"

In an instant. "Tomorrow," I said, laughing, pitching my hips against his. Pleasure burned low in my belly, roiling, growing. "I'd marry you tomorrow, Jackson."

"I'd make an honest man out of you," he said, hushed and low, and kissed me again.

For a moment, I didn't know who we were. We'd inhabited other selves, decided on impossible lives, became unrecognizable. I knew him, though. Knew the dark blush fanned across his nose, knew the soft moan creeping over his lips, knew the hand on my waist and the gasp he tried to stifle. The black, thorny tattoo on his stomach brushed the pouty skin beneath my navel. I wanted to stay there, suspended in unhurried sensuality. It was hot, building pleasure, steady and thick. Sex that felt eternal. Physicality that warmed and grew but didn't overwhelm. *So unlike us*, I thought. *More of this, more, more.*

Sometimes I forgot that our terrible, stolen love could be easy. Could heal. I held him as our bodies took precedence, as we chased each other to climax. I came first—*of course, of course*—with my gaze set on him, and my mouth trembling, whimpering and shaking and in love, God, in love, in love.

Jackson held himself above me, quickening his pace. I spread my legs and watched his expression tense, his jaw slacken, his brow furrow. Clenched around him and pushed myself closer, took his dick deeper, and smiled when he quivered and spurted, grinding the base of his cock hard against my slick cunt.

I drew him into a kiss. Ran my fingers through his hair and scraped my nails across his scalp, pressing my lips to his mouth, his cheek, the stubborn stubble on his jaw. He let his weight go heavy, still buried inside me, and maneuvered us onto our sides. I fit my thigh over his hip and hid beneath his chin, tracking the spidery tickle of his bony knuckles up and down my back.

The silence wasn't strained, but it wasn't simple either.

Jackson wasn't naive. He hadn't erased my pain for good—we both knew that—but comfort, and release, and adoration made the grief I'd been trapped in seem distant and small. The sweat on our skin dried. Breathing quieted. I pulled my face back to look at him, to see his sharp features dulled post-coital, and bumped my nose against his.

"It's almost over," he said.

"What?"

"Today. Shower, dinner, maybe we'll watch a movie, and then it's done. We'll wake up tomorrow and you'll marry me."

I laughed, sheepish and embarrassed. "You'd marry me, huh? You'd really do it?"

"If you let me."

"Think the world would write about us? Give us a quirky name."

The Cannibal Couple. Murderous Husbands. I thought about us on the cover of Times—*Queer Cuisine Gone Wrong!*—and in newspaper headlines—*faggots make a meal out of anyone*—and dictated strongly by well-spoken newscasters—*married couple in Aurora uncovered as killer cannibals, next at five.*

Jackson raised an eyebrow. "Likely, yeah. I'll never get caught, though. Not alive, at least."

Sometimes, I imagined us different. If we would've loved the mundane, mediocre versions of each other, or if it was our bloodlust that kept us together. If Jackson would've talked to me in the grocery store, or if I would've tried to buy him a drink at a bar. The way he said *I'll never get caught* instead of *we'll never get caught* made my heart skip, my pulse sputter. *Right*, I thought, *right, of course.* Because if we ever got caught, I'd be the one to kill him, and if we ever got caught, I'd be given a choice: die alongside him, put the blame on his corpse, or take the fall.

I didn't want to think about the *what if*. The crossroads we hadn't come to yet.

"Adrian Monroe," I said, sounding out a new life like a prayer.

"It suits you," Jackson said, and kissed me.

ADRIAN PRICE

It was half past midnight on the thirty-first of October and I could not see a thing.

The soft, satin blindfold fastened around my eyes was lightweight and comfortable. Heat filled the car. Music played. Something old. *Arctic Monkeys*, I think. The wheels jostled, leaving smooth asphalt for lumpy dirt. I braced on the dash. Jackson curled his palm around my thigh, steadying me. I swallowed, swiveling my head from side-to-side. It was instinct—the urge to establish sensory relevance—but there was no use. Light hardly slivered the bottom of the silky covering and darkness reigned everywhere else.

I knew three things, intimately.

One, we were going on a date. Non-negotiable.

Two, the date itself was a surprise. Mandatory.

Three, I was not allowed to know where we went, what we'd be doing, or how we got there.

Calm down, we're not going to the airport, he'd assured, securing the blindfold while we idled in the parking garage beneath his apartment. My anxiety would've skyrocketed had we boarded a spur-of-the-moment flight.

Those three things were all I had, though.

We spent the drive, all forty-five minutes of it, suspended in comfortable silence, listening to rain pelt the windshield and tunes whisper softly through the speakers. I mulled over what exactly he had in mind. Dinner, maybe. Or a party of some sort. I shifted in the seat, trailing my fingertips along the ridge of his bent knuckles. It'd been eighteen months since he'd taken me. Seventeen full moons. One anniversary. Two victims—chosen, hunted, butchered, bled, and cooked. One almost break up; our fight in July, summer sweltered, fireworks burst, and Jackson Monroe cried to me, bellowing about God, and punishment, and living without. *You're selfish*, he'd spat, words shaped like fists, *kill me, at least. Kill me and go.* We'd clawed at each other. Turned rabid and brutal, biting and scratching, bruising and swatting. I'd slept in the guestroom that night—the place where I'd first laid eyes on him—and he'd crawled into bed beside me at daybreak, whimpering about heartbreak, and marriage, and Eden.

I didn't leave, of course. The thought itself, the prospect of being without him, petrified me.

Three months had come and gone, but the fight felt fresh, somehow. It stayed. Lasted. Endured.

The car rolled to a stop. Headlights clicked. The engine died.

I inhaled deeply. "Jackson."

"Adrian," he replied, smooth as polished stone.

"Can I take this off now?"

"Not yet. I have to explain the rules first."

"Rules?"

He laughed in his throat. That sexy, rumbling sound. "Yes, rules. Are you listening?"

I nodded.

"Good. We're at the warehouse off Bramble and Sky Lodge." He released my thigh. Something rattled in the cupholder. "I'm setting a timer for three minutes. When it goes off, you'll remove the blindfold, get out of the car and go inside."

My pulse quickened. "And after that?"

"You'll run."

Chills scaled my spine. "And you'll—"

"Chase."

I turned toward him and reached for the blindfold, but he snatched my wrists, halting me.

"You want to *hunt* me, Jackson Monroe," I purred, swallowing a small, fragile laugh. I felt his breath on my face, coasting across my skin, warm and coffee-stained. "Is that what this is?"

I heard the smile in his voice. "If you make it through the maze, you get a prize."

"And if I don't?"

"Oh, if I catch you..." He let go of one wrist and cupped my face, thumbing at my mouth. He tugged at my bottom lip. Touched the tip of his finger to my front tooth. It was a strange, intimate thing. Him, like this. I'd missed it. "I get to do whatever I want."

I tried to speak, but he kissed me, fast a full, and then exited the 4Runner.

I should've expected something like this. Should've braced for a twisted game, or a murder mystery, or a theatrical performance of some sort. I reached for the silk and paused, seized by the command I'd nearly broken. *When it goes off, you'll remove the blindfold.* I waited, breath held, cycling through the game he'd planned and executed. The warehouse off Bramble and Sky Lodge... I tried to picture it in my head... A few miles off the main road, surrounded by wilderness, nestled behind a wooded area. I remembered a billboard advertisement. *Halloween Extravaganza! Think you can survive it?* I remembered checking the weather. Rain, constant. I remembered Jackson's outfit—charcoal pants, matte black button-down, laced moto-boots—and became hyperaware of my own cashmere sweater and plain denim.

Excitement fluttered in my belly. My chest lightened, my bones hummed, and I startled the moment my phone chimed. My heart leaped. I tore the blindfold off and threw it in the driver's seat, straining to see through the windshield. The rectangular building blurred beyond the wet glass. A door on the left was propped open, allowing red light to bleed out onto the walkway.

You'll run. His voice echoed, branded on the innerworkings of each thought. Heady excitement wormed through me. It felt like I'd been transported to the past, to those first few days, exploring his apartment, reading his journal, fearing him wholly, entirely.

Love had softened that bone chilling dread, though. Now, knowing Jackson Monroe had begged me, knowing I'd put my mouth to his tearstained cheek and tasted the prospect of *him* without *me*, knowing I was as monstrous as him, knowing he would die—*we would die*—without access to each other, without the promise of a shared tomorrow, turned fear into desire.

I was not afraid. But I wanted to be. I wanted Jackson to terrify me, and thrill me, and keep me.

Rain splattered my face and shoulders. I closed the car door and glanced around, jogging through the soaked grass to the side of the building. The closer I got, the more I understood. Noises erupted from inside the warehouse—haunting, melodic music, shrieks and witchy laughter, hydraulics and whirring fog machines. I peeked around the edge of the door before stepping inside.

The haunted house was empty of any attendees or scare actors, but the attraction itself was alive and well. The first room was a claustrophobic hallway, black-walled and dimly lit, leading to a corridor draped in thin, black fabric. I inhaled slowly and stepped forward, dragging my hand along the makeshift wall, pushing past the onyx tassels, and entering the first leg of the maze.

Like most haunted houses, this one was equipped with humorous animatronics. The smell of plastic and fog juice permeated the air, and lightbulbs were cleverly angled to keep the space basked in blackness.

The first room was designed to look like a hospital. Blood streaked the wall, surgical tools lie abandoned in a bloody tray, and an autopsied torso stretched across a silver table. Sticky faux blood puddled on the floor. I stepped over a person-sized zombie doll and gasped, jolting in place when another creature lurched upward from the floor. A loud growl shot through a nearby speaker. I hiccupped on a laugh, splaying one hand over my chest.

Where are you?

I crept into the next room.

The theme continued. More zombies—gaping jaws, bloodied mouths, sallow teeth, and rotting skin—filled the room. Latex limbs hung from the ceiling, bouncing off my shoulders and arms as I weaved through the room. A strobe light flickered, distorting the darkness. Fake zombies stood with their arms outstretched, filling the small space like mannequins. Out of the corner of my eye, one seemed to move. My pulse doubled. *There you are*, I thought. I stopped in my tracks. Stared at the corner where a figure had stood a second ago, hidden amidst the crowd of undead. The strobe flashed. Along the backwall, a familiar mask—painted like a skull—illuminated.

One blink, there. Another, gone. One blink, there, closer. Another, gone.

Something sharp graced my nape. Cold to the touch. His knife.

"When I said run, I meant *run*," Jackson said, suddenly behind me.

I sprang forward, dipping around zombies and shoving latex legs and arms out of the way. I wanted to laugh—I might've laughed, actually—but I ran, too. Into the next room, foggy and full of oozing green corpses, hopped over a fake manhole, gurgling with slime, and gasped when Jackson made a grab for my wrist. I yanked away. Kept going, into the next room, sprinting past an exorcist-style scene with a rendition of Regan MacNeil spraying pea soup onto a ruined bed. The speakers blasted a priest's frantic prayers. I paused, caught off guard by the crackling static cushioning *Holy Father* and *Lord, be with us* and *deliver your child*. I spun on my heels, assessing the room. A hole in the right-side wall-panel spat thick fog. The grayish smoke coiled around my ankles, bending like snakes as I took another few steps.

Something inside me had been triggered. Fight or flight. This overwrought need to be seen but to remain hidden, to be caught but to escape. Strange, to feel myself war between instinct and impulse. I was scared, but I wasn't. Electrified, almost. As if I'd stepped out of myself. Like the game of cat and mouse Jackson had planned for us had rewired my nervous system.

I was alight with it, that inclination toward danger, and shaky with excitement.

My body knew fear, viscerally, but I knew Jackson better.

A warm hand cuffed my wrist. I squeaked—*embarrassing*—and squirmed. As he yanked me backward, I smacked into his chest. Recognized his cologne. Knew the smooth line of his blade as the knife skimmed my throat.

I almost went limp. Almost let him have me. But I thrashed instead and ducked out from under his hold, wrenching my arm away. My knees wobbled. My legs trembled. I caught myself on the edge of the next doorway and ran through it into another dark room. Air shot from several holes drilled into the charcoal walls, hitting my face and body. I jerked to the side, triggering a screaming ghoul to hop from a hidden place. I swallowed the surprised noise gathering in my throat and kicked against the ground, propelling myself forward.

The next corridor was skinny and small, just a simple, metal walkway with guardrails. But around it, a huge, neon tube spun, splattered with different glowing colors, and a strobe repeatedly clicked, dizzying me. I stumbled across the walkway, tipping one way then the other, and finally made it across to the next room.

I didn't have time to catch my breath. Didn't have time to do anything except shout and dodge as Jackson closed in on me. The suddenness of him made my chest tighten and my stomach clench. He was the man I'd first seen in the apartment, standing in the doorway, haloed by the hall light. He was the man who stalked and hunted, the predator I'd found myself entrapped with for an eternity. He moved so quickly I couldn't parse it. I saw the crescent moon on his knuckle and flew backward. Saw the way his shoulders flexed, how his chest expanded on a deep inhale, and my body went rigid.

I was scared, of course. But the heat between my legs registered fear as something else, too.

Jackson could've had me. I knew what he was capable of, knew he could've taken two easy steps, made a few simple moves, and I would've been his. But I dodged again, and he let me, and I ran again, backward, toward the entrance of the maze, and he let me.

I made it through across the walkway, and almost through the exorcist room, but that was as far as I got.

Jackson grabbed me by the waist then reached around and sealed his hand around my neck, stopping me. I strained against him for a moment, but he didn't let me go.

"Too easy," he cooed, pressing his mask against my ear.

I swallowed hard. My lungs burned.

Carefully, Jackson brushed his hand along the waistband of my pants and thumbed open the button. The zipper dragged, so slowly. He pushed the denim down a few inches, scraped his knife over my panties and pressed the flat blade to my clothed cunt.

"You're shaking," he whispered. "Eager little whore."

Around us, the soundtrack of the priest played on a constant loop, overlayed with demonic vocals.

Heat rushed into my face. My groin clenched. I wanted to spread my legs, but I was trapped in my clothes. Wanted to expose myself, but Jackson wouldn't relent. He squeezed my throat and rubbed the knife back and forth. My jaw slackened. The barely lit room came in and out of focus.

"You'd let me, wouldn't you?" Jackson pulled the knife away and turned it over in his palm, working the handle against my slit. My underwear dampened. "You *would*," he purred. With a swipe of his index, he pushed my panties aside. "Knowing I've opened bodies with this..." He slid the black handle along my wet pussy, teasing at my hole. "Knowing what I've done with it..." Saliva pooled in my mouth. I sucked in a sharp breath, moaning at the initial breach. He worked the knife in small, shallow thrusts. The tool was big enough to drag inside me, to widen me, to fill me, but not long enough to reach deep, to satiate.

I knew it'd come to this. As soon as he'd mentioned the chase, as soon as he'd blindfolded me, as soon as he'd said *date*. But I couldn't get a grasp on my body's reaction. Didn't understand why the adrenaline made me weak and girlish, flushed from nose to feet and slick with *want*.

"Look at you," he said, twisting the handle inside me, rubbing it hard against my front wall. "Impaled on the murder weapon."

I made a guttural noise. My cunt spasmed and flooded.

The cool blade rested against my thigh, the base of it held between his thumb and pointer finger. He left the handle wedged inside me and brought his hand to my cock, framing the small, swollen nub. He circled the flesh there, spreading wetness. I moaned. The sound came up and out of me, loud and unrestrained. The hand around my throat loosened and he cupped the bottom of my chin. When I reached for the knife, hoping I could slide the handle deeper, he stopped me.

"You get a head start," he said, and eased the black handle free.

I turned, watching. He unwrapped his hand from around my neck, pulled down his mask and dragged his tongue from the tip of the blade to the bottom of the handle. What he said didn't register at first. I was too keyed up to recognize the warning in his voice, too feverish to look beyond the promise of pleasure.

Jackson pulled his mask up and nodded toward the next room. "Five... Four..."

I straightened in place and fixed my clothes.

"...Three... Two..."

And I forced myself to run.

My balance was off at first. I stumbled. Caught myself on the guardrail in the neon room and kept going, darting into the next dark, smoky segment. Fog juice pumped from the ceiling, charred skeletons and zombified animals snarled from the corners. I followed the glinting orange cinders along the wall to the next area, running through the room. A ghost flew down from the ceiling, cutting a white line across my path. I jumped to the side and kept going, mind still fuzzy, body still humming, and yelped the moment Jackson stepped out of the shadows in front of me.

Another strobe, slower, meant to exasperate the dark, clicked on and off. He closed the space between us and shot his hand out, taking the back of my skull. He threaded his hand through my hair and gripped.

"Down," he commanded.

I sank to my knees.

"Obedience is a beautiful thing." Jackson peered at me over the thin, fabric edge of his half-mask. His eyes were dark and sharp—the only human thing about him. He brought the knife to my face, allowing the blade to concave my flesh but didn't press hard enough to cut. "Open," he said, sliding the knife over the center of my mouth. The tip bounced off my tooth and caught my bottom lip. I ignored the sting and did as I was told.

Jackson sheathed the knife on the holster clipped to his belt and flicked the button on his pants.

"*Open*," he repeated.

I stretched my jaw, gaping.

"Good," he rasped, thrusting into my mouth. His cock ran across my tongue and slipped down my throat. I gripped the bunched fabric above his knees and kept my eyes open, watching his skeletal face.

I was so wet. My cunt ached, my body quivered, I wanted desperately—to touch myself, for him to touch me. I could think of nothing else as he grunted and pumped his cock between my lips, crowding my throat, ignoring my slippery gurgles and soupy whines. He tightened his hold on my hair and held me still, pressing his pelvis against my nose. My throat constricted on a painful gag, closing around him, and saliva strung from my chin.

Jackson pulled back and rested the head of his cock on my tongue. I stretched my mouth. Drool coated my lips, tears clouded my eyes, but I gave myself over to him and waited. The strobe flashed. Harsh white light came and went, intensifying his sharp features. His chest rose and fell.

"I really wanted to get to the exam room," Jackson said. He sounded much less put together than he had before. His voice wavered, verging on playful. An accidental laugh came and went.

Oh. I smiled and closed my lips around his cock, sucking lazily. *Guess the hunt is over.*

"Stop, stop," he said. "I wanted to fuck you on this... this table—I had a whole plan."

"Did you catch me too quickly?" I asked, running my lips across his shaft.

He nodded vigorously. "Got ahead of myself."

I stood and wiped my mouth with the back of my hand. He tucked himself into his pants and crowded me backward, walking us toward the next room. We stumbled through different parts of the maze, hands roaming, tugging at clothes, eyes alight, making sure we didn't trip over props. We crossed through a threshold, and I tugged at his mask, pulling it down, exposing his mouth. The fear, thrill, electricity hadn't faded. The urge to have him—this Jackson, the man who'd taken me, who shared my bed—was too strong to ignore.

I went hot against him and shoved my hands beneath his shirt, feeling across the thorny black ink on his stomach. Jackson kissed me deeply, like he was starved for it, like we hadn't seen each other in months. And maybe we hadn't. Maybe that gritty, explosive fight had turned our summer into a detour and this was us coming back to each other. I'd forgiven him for the ugliness the day after we'd fought, and he'd forgiven me, I'm sure, but we'd tiptoed around each other, afraid we might detonate in the aftermath of explosive insecurity. Sex had been thoughtless lately. Careful and unlike us. At times, we'd fucked with misunderstood hunger, using each other for release and comfort, but the passion was closed-off. It made me miss him. The whole of him—*this* version of him. We'd given each other enough space to get right, to digest our own proximity to annihilation, and Jackson was finally making the executive decision to say *enough*.

I loved him even more for it, somehow.

Jackson stopped us in the next room. It was another hospital set, but this one was rigged with multiple surgical tables and an assortment of flayed open corpses. He shoved a rubber zombie off a nearby examination table and took me by the waist, lifting me up onto the metal surface.

"Come here," he said, even though I was right there, reaching for him, tugging him closer. His voice was raspy and rich, melting into my mouth during another deep, fluid kiss.

I lifted when he prompted me to and shimmied out of my pants. I was too eager to strip completely, so the garment clung to my calf and hung around my right shoe. Jackson yanked my underwear to the side and slid into me on a rushed thrust, burying his cock deep. We were clumsy about it, fucking like teenagers, like we'd entered a chase, like I couldn't get enough of him, like he couldn't fathom separating from me. It was fast and reckless. Jackson snaked his hand around my waist and snapped his hips, pistoning, driving himself deeper, faster. I braced with one palm on the table, the other squeezing the slight curve where his throat met his shoulder, and accepted his punishing pace. Heat grew in my stomach. I kept my eyes on him. Watched his mouth drop open, and his breath come short, and his brow cinch. Pleasure was a ruthless thing like this. His body; mine. The tension built and burned, settling like a pleasant ache between my hip bones.

I wanted him to tear me apart. I wanted him to hold me.

What a strange, primal thing to crave desecration and devotion at once.

I scraped my bottom lip with my teeth, biting to ground myself, to swallow an inkling of pain. The second I did, Jackson pushed me backward, splaying me across the table. He collared me with his palm, wrapping his wide hand around my throat with such ease, and dug his blunt fingertips into my hip.

"What do you want?" Jackson asked.

My lashes fluttered. I whined, gushing around his cock.

"Say it," he demanded.

I spread my legs. "Harder."

"Again."

"Harder, please—"

Jackson slammed his hips against mine. It jostled me. Caused the table to rock and shake. I cried out and bent away from the cool surface, secured by his hand, impaled on his dick, completely at his mercy. It was too loud, too riddled with recorded screams and eerie graveyard music. I couldn't hear what we sounded like—our bodies meeting—but I felt the soaked friction between us, knew the sweat on the back of my thighs and the slick spread around the base of his cock, imagined every wet *slap* echoing through the maze, lost to the horror noises and zombie groans.

His thumb circled my swollen cock. I wanted to hold off, to last longer, but my body relented. I gaped at the ceiling, arching away from the table, and gasped at the sudden onslaught of pleasure. Every muscle clenched. Everything wound tight, *tighter*, and broke with a quickness I hadn't anticipated. I spasmed and clenched, squirted and gushed. My hips shook. Vision blurred and trembled. I heard him curse. Felt him press between my legs, buried deep, and grind against my clit. His grip on my waist turned to iron, and he squeezed my neck a little tighter.

Heat flooded inside me. He made a wounded noise when he came, leaning over me, eyes hazy and dark, lips parted and reddened.

Before the fuzzy heat left each of my limbs, Jackson let go of my throat and rested his hand on my face, thumbing gently at my cheekbone. It'd been weeks since he'd touched me like that. Tenderly, sewn with love. Sometimes in the night, I'd wake to find him curled against me, softened by sleep, holding onto my ribcage or hipbone, but this was the first time he'd touched me fully, purposefully, without flinching away.

It was as if Jackson Monroe had been afraid to press his love into the places he'd once kissed, and nuzzled, and licked, and bitten. And I'd been scared, too, I think. Afraid I might love him too hard. This is what it was to be with him, for him to be with me. We were shackled to each other, miserably in love, and neither one of us had the strength to undo it.

Love was where we would rot. Like this, like we had in July, like we did upon meeting.

And one day, it would certainly kill us.

I leaned into his hand and turned, pressing my mouth to the center of his palm.

"You *are*," he said, as if he'd realized something.

I leaned forward. He took my weight, hauling me closer. Our noses brushed. I felt his breath, the soft scrape of his mask on my jaw, and saw something new in his eyes. Devastation. Finality.

"I'm what?"

"My own personal haunting. My bad miracle." He kissed me once, gently, then again, rougher, hungrier.

I am, I almost said, but I kept kissing him instead. Kept holding onto him.

It was Halloween, and the veil was thin, and I knew love like a dog-bite, like a car wreck, like a prodigy, like a ghost, like a baptism. I knew love like Jackson Monroe, and he knew love like mine—undying.

I knew love. *I knew love.*

SAINT HARLOWE

you can call me **saint** or **ghost**. i'm a transmasc writer peddling filthy notgood stories about the gross stuff we sometimes get off on. i like to write about people becoming gods and gods becoming people. how we consume and undo each other.

thank you for loving my badboys.

content warnings for all my work can be found on my website: https://saintharlowe.carrd.co/

Printed in Great Britain
by Amazon